# CARLA CASSIDY

## SCENE OF THE CRIME: MYSTIC LAKE

D0556630

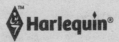

TORONTO NEW YORK LONDON
AMSTERDAM PARIS SYDNEY HAMBURG
STOCKHOLM ATHENS TOKYO MILAN MADRID
PRAGUE WARSAW BUDAPEST AUCKLAND

To Jackie, who gave me two beautiful grandchildren
and, for the last four months, has kept my coffee cup full
while I work. Thanks and I love you.

Recycling programs
for this product may
not exist in your area.

ISBN-13: 978-0-373-69597-3

SCENE OF THE CRIME: MYSTIC LAKE

Copyright © 2012 by Carla Bracale

## "This shook you up pretty badly," Cole said softly.

Her gaze met his. "I'd be lying if I said anything else." She sank down on the edge of the bed and set her bag next to her. "Seeing it right here, in the place where I live, in the place where my son sleeps and eats. I don't think I've really processed it until now, while I'm packing up to leave everything."

"It's going to be all right," he said as he shifted from one foot to the other. "We're going to get this guy."

She nodded, her head still down. She looked momentarily broken and he ached for her. Since the moment he'd met her, she'd radiated an inner strength, a wealth of spirit that had drawn him to her. But he found himself equally as drawn to the woman seated on the bed who looked like she needed nothing more than a pair of strong arms around her.

He walked over to stand directly in front of her. "Amberly," he said softly.

She looked up at him then and her beautiful brown eyes were filled with tears. He opened his arms and she shot off the bed and into them as if she'd just been waiting for him to make the offer.

## ABOUT THE AUTHOR

Carla Cassidy is an award-winning author who has written more than fifty novels for Harlequin Books. In 1995, she won Best Silhouette Romance from *RT Book Reviews* for *Anything for Danny*. In 1998, she also won a Career Achievement Award for Best Innovative Series from *RT Book Reviews*.

Carla believes the only thing better than curling up with a good book to read is sitting down at the computer with a good story to write. She's looking forward to writing many more books and bringing hours of pleasure to readers.

### Books by Carla Cassidy

# CAST OF CHARACTERS

*Cole Caldwell*—Sheriff of Mystic Lake and not thrilled to be working with the beautiful Amberly Nightsong.

*Amberly Nightsong*—A Native American FBI agent who comes to Mystic Lake to help solve three murders with ritualistic overtones.

*Max Nightsong*—Amberly's bright and loving six-year-old son.

*John Merriweather*—Amberly's ex-husband and a successful Western painter, who is having difficulty letting go of the Indian princess he'd considered his muse.

*Jeff Maynard*—A bartender who dated the first victim. He's a hothead with a nasty reputation.

*Raymond Ross*—A ladies' man and friend of Jeff's, who provided his friend an alibi for the night of the murder. Is it possible he not only lied, but also participated in the murders?

*Jimmy Tanner*—It's rumored his marriage is on the rocks and he had a brief affair with one of the victims. Did he kill her to save his marriage?

# Chapter One

Amberly Nightsong watched the children pouring out of the grade school, the variety of shapes and sizes and colors decorating the last of the summer grass as they raced to awaiting school buses and parked cars.

As always, her heart swelled as she saw the small, slender dark-haired boy running toward her, his face lit with a beatific smile. Max. At six years old, he owned her heart in a way no other male ever had before.

He opened up the passenger door, threw his bright blue backpack onto the backseat and then got into the car. "Hi, Mom."

"Hi, Max, how was your day?" she asked as she waited for him to buckle in and then pulled away from the curb.

"Good, except for at recess Billy Stamford called me a sissy boy because I wear a necklace."

Amberly glanced over at her son and the necklace she'd placed around his neck when he was three years old. It was the same necklace Amberly's grandmother had placed around her neck when she'd been three years old.

The silver owl had been hand pounded and crafted by her grandfather and was a talisman against evil. The rawhide string that it hung from had been replaced many times over the years, and even though Amberly didn't live the Cherokee way of her ancestors, when she'd draped it around Max's neck, she'd figured a lucky charm from her grandfather, intended for protection, couldn't hurt.

"Did you tell him it isn't just any necklace but a very special protection necklace? Did you explain to him that the owl and the cougar were the only creatures that stayed awake for the entire seven days of Creation?" she asked.

"Nah, I just told him he was a poo-head, and then we played baseball."

Amberly bit back a smile, wishing all conflicts could be resolved so easily. But as an FBI profiler, she knew that wasn't the way life worked. Conflicts got messy and people could be twisted, and by the time she was called to work a case, somebody was almost always dead.

"I'm ready whenever you are," Max said, a touch of eagerness in his voice.

"Okay." Amberly slowed the car a bit as they drove by a coffee shop where several people were seated outside, enjoying the early-September sun. "The man in the red shirt," she said. Their car drove slowly past the shop, and then she stepped on the gas. "Go."

Max frowned thoughtfully and then began. "His shirt was red and he had on blue jeans. One knee was ripped out and he had on blue-and-white sneakers. He had blond hair and a mustache."

"Excellent, Max," Amberly said proudly. "You're going to be the best FBI agent in the whole world whcn you get old enough."

It was a game they played every day on the way home from school, honing his powers of observation. He loved it, especially when he noticed something about somebody or someplace that she hadn't noticed at all.

They were almost home when her cell phone beeped to indicate a text message. She dug it out of her purse and frowned.

"Looks like I'll be going to Dad's," Max said as he saw her expression.

"Looks like," she agreed and hit one on her speed dial. Her ex-husband, John, answered on the second ring. "What's up?" His deep voice, as always, whispered an edge of guilt through her.

"I just picked Max up from school and then got a message that I need to go in."

"Bring him by. Tell him we'll order pepperoni pizza for dinner."

"Okay, be there in ten." She clicked off and glanced at Max. "Dad said he'll order pepperoni pizza for supper."

"Awesome, that's my favorite. Am I going to spend the night there?"

"Hopefully not, but you know how this goes. I need to find out what's going on, and then I'll call later and let you know the plan."

"Okay," Max agreed easily.

Amberly thanked the stars that when she and John had divorced four years ago they had remained close friends, both committed to maintaining a healthy relationship for Max's sake. She was also incredibly lucky that John worked from home and was always available to keep Max, as her work hours were so unpredictable.

Within ten minutes, she pulled into the driveway of the neat ranch house where she had once lived as John Merriweather's wife. She'd kept her maiden name when they married as an honor to Granny Nightsong, the grandmother who had raised her. Max was a Merriweather by name, but definitely a Nightsong in spirit.

John greeted them at the door, his handsome face wreathed in a smile as he gave Max a fist pump and then smiled at Amberly. "Just dinner or overnight?"

"I don't know yet. I got a text to see Director Forbes as soon as possible. I'm not assigned right now to anything specific, so I have no idea what to expect. I'll call you?"

"We'll be here," he said as he scuffed the top of Max's gleaming black hair.

Twenty minutes later, Amberly walked into the downtown Kansas City FBI building. She flashed her badge and identification to the security guard on duty, despite the fact that she'd been coming into the office at least five days a week for the past eight years, since four weeks after her twenty-second birthday.

The passion she should have felt for John when they'd married had always been superseded by her passion for her job. She'd known in her heart as she'd walked down the wedding aisle that she was making a mistake, but three months pregnant and desperate to create a family unit for the baby she carried, she'd said "I do."

For the next three years she had tried to make it work. But she'd known her own unhappiness with the marriage and had sensed John's. Ultimately, she'd left the marriage behind when Max was two, with the determination to keep the divorce as friendly and healthy for her son as possible.

All thoughts of John and her failed marriage fled her head as she knocked on Director Daniel Forbes's door. "Enter," his deep voice boomed.

She opened the door to see her boss seated at his desk. Even sitting, he was an imposing figure with his steel-gray hair and matching eyes.

"Agent Nightsong." He gestured her into the chair in front of his desk. "Mystic Lake."

Amberly blinked. It always took her a minute or two to adjust to Director Forbes's form of abrupt communication. There were times she wasn't sure if he knew nouns and verbs could be used to form a complete sentence. She waited for him to continue.

"You know it?"

"Not well. Small town about twenty miles from here." When she was with Director Forbes she found herself talking in sentence fragments, as well, as if he had a communication disease that was contagious. "Problems?"

"Three murders. Ritualistic overtones. The third victim was found forty-five minutes ago."

"Have we been invited in?" Amberly asked.

Forbes frowned, a deep vertical cut appearing in the center. "The mayor called me. Doesn't want us in officially but would like somebody there to unofficially aid law enforcement."

"So, local law enforcement isn't eager."

"That's probably an understatement," he replied. "You're assigned in a consulting capacity, and they're holding the latest scene for your arrival. It's in the city park. Your contact is Sheriff Cole Caldwell." He gave a curt nod of his head toward the door, his official dismissal.

Minutes later, Amberly was back in her car and headed to the small town of Mystic Lake. All she knew about the little town was that it was built at the edge of a small lake and that its Main Street had a reputation for quaint antique shops, crafty boutiques and intriguing eateries, which drew tourists during the summer months.

As she drove, she reached into the center section of her car console and withdrew a length of red licorice from a package she kept stashed there. She'd quit smoking on the day she'd found out she was pregnant with Max, changing that addiction to one for red licorice.

Sheriff Cole Caldwell. She chewed thoughtfully. She could just imagine what she would be up against, some good old boy who ran the place with an iron fist and wore a fat belt buckle to hold in his immense beer belly.

In her experience, small-town sheriffs hated two things—anyone questioning their authority and FBI agents. She glanced at her watch. It was already almost five. She might as well give John a call and tell him it was going to be an overnighter with Max.

She had no idea what she was walking into, but if it was serial kills with ritualistic overtones, then she had a feeling there were going to be a lot of overnighters with John for Max in the near future.

She took the highway exit that would lead to the town north of Kansas City. One of the things she loved about this city was the fact that within a fifteen-minute drive, you could be out of the concrete jungle and into rolling pastures and shady woodlands.

There were times she thought about moving out here, someplace outside the city limits, where Max could have room to maybe have a horse, but she couldn't discount the convenience of having John living a mere three blocks from the small house where she and Max now lived.

As she turned onto Main Street of Mystic Lake she wondered where, exactly, the city park might be. As she looked up and down each side street she passed, she steeled herself for joining a party where she was, in effect, an uninvited and unwanted guest.

"The willow tree bends but rarely breaks in the force of a gale." It was Granny Nightsong's voice that whispered through her head. Amberly smiled, the warmth of her memory tempered by grief.

Granny Nightsong had been a curious blend of Cherokee and flat-out crazy. Although she'd passed some of the traditions of her heritage to Amberly, Granny was also prone to making up legends and old, wise sayings to fit the circumstance. When Granny had taught Amberly the Stomp Dance of their people, Amberly had recognized more than a little bit of jitterbug in it.

Granny Nightsong fled from her mind as she looked down a side street and spied what appeared to be the city park. As she turned and headed in that direction, she knew she was right. Yellow crime-scene tape was strung from one tree to another, and several official cars were parked in the graveled lot.

She pulled up next to them and got out of her car, immediately halted by a stern-faced young deputy. "Crime scene working, nobody is allowed in this area," he said.

She flashed her badge and continued forward. As she got closer to the scene, her mind processed several things at one time…the victim, a pretty, blond-haired young woman, lay beneath the overhanging branches of a tree, and in the tree limb above her head was a bright red-and-yellow dream catcher…and Sheriff Cole Caldwell was a tall, dark-haired hottie without a belly bulge in sight as he leaned closer to the dream catcher for a better look.

He suddenly snapped his head around as if he'd somehow sensed her approach. She had one instant of noticing strong, handsome features before they twisted with anger and the blue of his eyes went icy cold as he straightened to his full height.

"Lady, can't you see this is a crime scene? Deputy Walkins, escort this woman away from here." His voice was deep, authoritative, as if he was accustomed to people jumping immediately to obey his orders.

Amberly held up a hand to stop the deputy, who moved toward her with a sense of purpose. She showed her identification and flashed the sheriff a bright smile. "Don't worry, I might look like a Native American, but actually I'm the Cavalry sent to save the day."

It was at that moment that she realized Sheriff Cole Caldwell had absolutely no sense of humor.

"*I* DIDN'T CALL FOR FBI assistance," Cole said. Cole hadn't been fond of the FBI since they'd botched a kidnapping job eight years ago that had resulted in the murder of his wife. "It was our mayor who called." And that call had held up the entire process while they all stood around and waited for Ms. I'm-Going-To-Fix-Your-Work-FBI-Agent to arrive.

"Yeah, I wasn't exactly expecting the welcome wagon to be drawn up for me," she replied dryly. "Agent Amberly Nightsong," she said and held out a hand to him.

"Sheriff Cole Caldwell." Her skin was soft, but her handshake was firm.

One thing was clear: the FBI agents of his memory were nothing like the stunning woman standing before him. It was obvious she was Native American. Her skin was a dusty bronze, and her cheekbones were high and well-defined.

She had doe eyes, round and dark and long lashed, and her hair was a rich, deep black that was captured in a braid that fell down the length of her back.

Worn jeans hugged long legs, and the bright yellow T-shirt she wore seemed to make her eyes darker and her skin glow with an inner light.

She took a step closer to the victim, and he watched her through narrowed eyes. "First of all, I'm not sure what your thinking is, but no self-respecting Native American would have done this and left those cheap Made In China dream catchers at the scene," she said.

In truth, he'd wondered if perhaps the perp was a Native American, but he wasn't about to admit that to her. "You have an ID?" she asked.

"Victim is twenty-seven-year-old Barbara Tillman."

"A local?" she asked.

Cole nodded. "She worked as a teacher's aide at the

grade school and lived in an apartment complex just off Main Street."

"And there have been two others before her?"

A fire of frustration burned in Cole's gut as he nodded once again. "Twenty-six-year-old Gretchen Johnson was found in front of a trash can next to a pizza place, and twenty-five-year-old Mary Mathis was found in front of the library."

"And dream catchers were hung at all three scenes?"

"Yes. When Gretchen Johnson was found, my first suspect was her boyfriend, but I couldn't break his alibi for the time of death. Then Mary showed up. Both women had been stabbed multiple times at some unknown location, then left at the sites, and the dream catchers were hung at both scenes. Both bodies had Taser marks and indications that they'd been bound and gagged."

"So, he Tasers them to incapacitate them and then ties them up and takes them someplace else, where he stabs them and then stages the dump scene with the dream catchers." She frowned thoughtfully. "And how long has it been since Mary's murder?"

"Two weeks. And it was four weeks between Gretchen's and Mary's murders. Have you seen enough? I'd like to start processing the scene. We haven't even allowed the coroner in yet."

"Knock yourself out," she said with a step backward.

As the coroner, a fat, balding man named George Thompson, moved in to assess time and method of death, Cole called to the three deputies who he'd meticulously trained in crime-scene procedure.

He gathered them in a group just far enough from where Agent Nightsong stood that he hoped she wouldn't hear the conversation. "Do your jobs and do them well," he said in a low voice. "I don't want any mistakes." Especially with the eyes of the FBI watching…judging their every move.

Once the coroner was finished with his examination of the body, he announced that he believed the murder had occurred at some point the night before, probably between the hours of midnight and three. Method of death was obvious, multiple stab wounds to the chest. He then stepped back to allow the deputies to begin their work.

Cole moved to stand next to Agent Nightsong. Beneath the odor of death that hung in the still air, he could smell the faint scent of her, a welcome smell of blooming exotic flowers.

The scent, so distinctly feminine and wafting from such a beautiful woman, stirred him on a base level that made him slightly uncomfortable.

"I suppose you already have a profile of the killer, neatly tied up with a bow," he said, vaguely aware that he sounded a bit surly.

She turned to look at him, her eyes filled with an edge of amusement. "You aren't the vision of a small-town sheriff that I had in mind while I was driving here, and hopefully you'll discover I'm not the uptight, upright FBI agent that you assume I am."

He narrowed his gaze as he stared at her. "And what vision did you entertain of me on your drive here?"

"Definitely shorter and rounder." She turned her attention to his men, meticulously moving around the crime scene with evidence bags and tweezers, their feet covered in booties. "I anticipated nobody who knew the first clue about a murder investigation, because I doubt if you see much of this kind of crime in this size of town, but it looks like your men all know what they're doing."

He didn't know if she expected him to be pleased about her assessment of him or his men's work. To be perfectly honest, he didn't much give a good damn about what she thought.

"And no," she continued, "I don't have a profile all neatly tied up with a bow in my head. It's far too early in the game for a full profile. Once this scene has been processed, I'd like copies of the files of the other two murders."

"Once we're finished up here, you can follow me to the office, and I'll see to it that you get copies." He was confident she would find nothing wrong with the way he'd conducted his investigations so far.

Unfortunately, there weren't many leads to follow at the moment. He'd already had one of his deputies find out the availability of the dream catchers and discovered that they were sold in most dollar stores and some craft and hobby shops in and around the area.

"The dream catchers...they're supposed to keep bad dreams away or something like that, right?"

She smiled and the beauty of that gesture shot an unexpected heat through Cole. It had been years since he'd allowed himself to feel anything for any woman, and the fact that a little lick of lust stirred in him for *this* woman didn't improve his mood at all.

"The legend is that the dream catcher was used by the

Woodland Indians to catch all dreams, both good and bad. The bad dreams get caught in the webbing and burn off with the morning sun. The good dreams are caught and make their way to the hole in the center, where they filter down the feathers and are dreamed."

He looked back at the victim and the dream catcher hanging over her head. "So, our perp wants to make sure our victims have only good dreams in death?"

"Or he wants you to believe that he's of Native American descent," she replied.

"But you don't think he is," he countered.

She frowned thoughtfully. "At this point, there's no way of really knowing. Certainly most Native Americans I know who own dream catchers have the real thing made with their own hands with either soaked willow or grapevine. They're usually very personal and made with lots of love." She flashed him another quick smile. "But of course, that's the old way."

He wondered if the FBI powers-that-be had specifically chosen her for this job because of her Native American background.

They fell quiet as the men continued their jobs, and the victim was eventually taken away. It was growing dark when the last of the work was done at the scene of the crime, and Agent Nightsong followed Cole to the sheriff's office.

He'd found her an irritant all evening. It wasn't anything she'd said. For the most part, she'd been silent. It had been the way she'd watched them with those intelligent, enigmatic eyes.

Cole had found himself snapping at his men, feeling

as if both he and all of them were on display and Agent Nightsong was just waiting for errors to occur so she could step in and take over.

As he drove toward the office, with her in her own car just behind him, he drew in a deep breath to ease the tension that had crackled through him since the moment she'd arrived on scene.

He wasn't arrogant enough to believe he didn't need some kind of help. This latest murder had definitely shaken him up. Not only did he lack the manpower for the kind of investigation these murders required, but he also lacked resources. Mystic Lake was a small town with very little crime, and it had been years since Cole had done the kind of police work that was now required of him.

He probably would have asked for help, but it ticked him off that the mayor hadn't even discussed the issue with him and instead had just gone behind Cole's back and then told him he'd called the feds.

As far as Cole was concerned, it had shown a lack of respect, which heated his insides along with the other feeling that fired inside him each time his gaze landed on Amberly Nightsong.

He'd give her the copies of the files of the other murders, and then she'd be on her way back to Kansas City. She wasn't officially a part of the case. She was just here as a consultant of sorts. She'd read the files, call him with her thoughts, and that would be the end of it.

His hands relaxed on the steering wheel as he turned into the parking lot behind his office. Funny that his lust hormones hadn't been active for eight long years and now had suddenly decided to awaken for the one woman he wanted absolutely nothing to do with.

She parked beside his car and joined him at the back door of the building. "It should take about twenty minutes or so to get copies of those files ready for you," he said as he used his key to unlock the back door of the building.

He gestured her into the hallway. A door on the left led to a conference room, a second to a small break room, and to the right was his private office. There was also an interrogation room. Ahead were the reception area and the deputy desks, with the jail in the basement of the building.

He took her into the conference room, where the old wall-size bulletin board was covered with crime photos of the two previous murders. It had become their war room, devoted specifically to the murders since the second one had occurred.

"If you'll wait here, I'll be back with copies of the files," he said.

She nodded absently, already engrossed in the photos on the board.

She was still standing in front of the board when he reentered the room fifteen minutes later. She appeared to be so deep in thought she didn't hear his return.

He took a brief moment to admire the curve of her butt in her tight jeans, the waist-length braided rope of thick hair that seemed to beg to be released from its binding. He cleared his throat, not liking the drift of his thoughts.

She whirled around to face him. "I can't help but wonder if there isn't some sort of a mercy-killing element to these. He killed them and then tried to assure that they would have happy dreams through eternity. Were any of the women sick? Maybe terminally ill?"

"According to the autopsy reports, both Mary Mathis and Gretchen Johnson were in perfect health, and of course we won't know about Barbara Tillman until George performs the complete autopsy. I should have something from him by midday tomorrow."

She frowned. "Well, that shoots my potential initial theory right out the window." She smiled. "But then it isn't unusual for me to throw out several of my theories before settling on the one that's right."

The room was too small and filled with that evocative scent of her. He was suddenly far too focused on her lips, which were covered with a nude, glossy lipstick. He should be thinking about the photos of the victims on the board, not the vibrant, beautiful woman in front of him.

"Here are the files," he said briskly and thrust them toward her. He wanted her gone, away from him. She unsettled him in a way that was distinctly uncomfortable.

"Thanks. Once I plow through these, I'll feel like I'm up to speed."

He gestured her out of the conference room and down the hallway toward the front of the building. When they reached the main area, he introduced her to Linda Scott, who served as receptionist/secretary and dispatcher.

"Where do you send your forensic evidence for analysis?" she asked when they stepped out the front door and into the warm September night.

"We use a lab in Kansas City. We don't have any facilities here."

"I could get you access to the FBI lab."

"That's not necessary," he replied. "I'm satisfied with the lab we're already using."

She shrugged her shoulders. "Suit yourself."

"Do you sleep under a dream catcher?" he asked, the personal question leaping from his mouth before he'd actually considered asking.

"My son does. The day he was born my granny Nightsong made him one to hang above his bed. I don't sleep beneath one." Her chocolate-brown eyes seemed to grow a tad bit darker. "I need to allow myself to have nightmares. It's one of the ways I get in touch with people who do things like this." She held up the files.

"You must have terrible dreams," he observed.

"Sometimes I do. I'll talk to you tomorrow."

He watched as she got into her car. He wasn't surprised that she had a family. A woman as bright as her, as beautiful as her, would have been snapped up by some man as quickly as possible.

As her car disappeared in the distance, he felt a touch of relief that she was definitely off-limits. Not that he was interested, not that he cared.

Cole had locked his heart away eight years ago when he'd lost his wife and every dream he'd ever entertained of being a husband and a father, and he had no intention of ever unlocking it.

If he was lucky he wouldn't see Agent Amberly Nightsong again. She'd phone in a report to him and that would be the end of her involvement in this case.

He turned on his heels and headed back into the office. He had three murders to solve and didn't have time to entertain thoughts of a hot-looking, married FBI agent who, for a moment, had stirred emotions long dead inside him...emotions he intended to remain dead for the rest of his life.

# Chapter Two

Amberly swigged the last of the coffee in her cup and then got up from her table as she eyed the microwave clock. Almost seven-thirty. She needed to get out of here if she wanted to stop by John's house and see Max before he left for school.

She grabbed the files that had kept her up most of the night and her purse and then left the house. As she drove the three blocks, she tried to slough off the exhaustion of a night of too little sleep.

These murders in Mystic Lake had already grabbed her by the throat, and she had a feeling they wouldn't let her go until somebody was behind bars.

She'd always been grateful that she usually had a level of detachment to the cases she worked that made her most effective and allowed her to leave the crime and the crime scene at work, keeping it from bleeding into her personal life.

These crimes felt different already. As she'd gone through the files she'd been unable to maintain that emotional distance that had always made things easier.

Maybe it was because the victims were not much younger than her own thirty years of age. Maybe it was the brutality alongside the beauty of the dream catcher, which was such a part of her heritage.

She shoved all thoughts of the files and the murder victims out of her mind as she pulled into John's driveway.

For the next few minutes, her thoughts and attention would be solely focused on Max. He greeted her at the front door, dressed for school in a pair of jean shorts and a white-and-red-striped pullover shirt. She fought the impulse to reach out and tamp down the cowlick at the back of his head.

"Mom," he said in surprise and threw himself into her arms.

Amberly hugged him tight, knowing that all too quickly the day would come when he would think it was uncool for his mommy to hug him. "I didn't know you were coming here this morning," he said as they finally disengaged from each other.

"I couldn't start my day without seeing my favorite boy," she replied. "Where's your dad?"

"In the kitchen, making French toast. You gonna eat with us?"

"I'm not hungry, but it sure smells good."

John appeared in the kitchen doorway. "Bacon and French toast, and I've got plenty."

"Thanks, but no. However, I wouldn't turn down a quick cup of coffee while you two eat."

He gestured with the pancake turner in his hand. "Come on, then. Max, wash your hands, it's on the table."

As Max ran for the bathroom, Amberly followed

John into the kitchen. He pointed her to a chair and then poured her a cup of coffee. "You look tired," he said.

"Late night. There's a serial murderer working in Mystic Lake, and I've been assigned to consult." She told him no more, having learned early in their marriage that John didn't want to hear about her work as a profiler.

John was an artist who'd made his name painting Western pictures with a glow of splendor. His world was one of beauty and history, and he'd never wanted her to bring the ugliness of her world inside their home.

At that moment, Max returned to the kitchen and slid into the chair where his breakfast awaited. As he ate, he chattered about the math test his dad had helped him study for the night before, his dream that he was riding in a car and excited about where they were going but being disappointed when he woke up before they'd arrived at their destination. By then it was time for Max to brush his teeth and finish getting ready for school.

"Thanks for the coffee," Amberly said to John as he walked her to the front door.

"Anytime. So, I'm assuming we're going to play things by ear when it comes to where Max is staying."

Amberly nodded. "I just don't have a good handle right now on where this is all going to lead. My plan right now is to be home by five or so tonight. If you can pick up Max from school, then I'll try to be here around then to pick him up and take him back to my place for the night."

John nodded. "Just let me know. You know I love it when he's here." There was a slight censure in his voice, as if what he wanted to say was that they all should be together under this roof, still a united family.

"Thanks again, John. I'll be in touch." She left, refusing to shoulder the guilt he'd subtly tried to put on her. As much as she would have loved for Max to have a mother and father that were together, the marriage hadn't worked. She and John should have remained good friends and never crossed the line into intimacy.

As she pulled out of the driveway to head to Mystic Lake her thoughts returned to the files in the seat next to her. One thing was clear after reading the reports and interviews that had been conducted after each murder: Cole Caldwell was good. In fact, he was better than good.

As she made the drive to the small town, she played and replayed the information she'd read the night before. Building a profile of a killer wasn't an easy task. Not only did the method of kill and the crime scene hold clues to coming up with a working profile, but the victims and their lives usually held clues, as well.

By the time she reached Mystic Lake and found a parking place in front of the sheriff's office, she was wishing for another cup of coffee to help jolt her into full-performance level.

She was dressed less casually today, clad in a pair of black slacks and a short-sleeved white button-down blouse. She'd been caught off guard yesterday, but today she felt more prepared to look and act the role of FBI consultant.

She entered the office and smiled at the woman Cole had introduced to her the night before. "Hi, Linda, is Sheriff Caldwell in?"

"I'm Lana, Linda's twin sister. She works nights and I work days. And you are?" She raised one of her dark eyebrows.

"Special Agent Amberly Nightsong."

"Is Sheriff Caldwell expecting you?" There was an obvious protective tone in her voice.

"I'm not sure if he is or not, but I'm here," Amberly replied.

"I'll see if he's available." She picked up the phone and swirled her chair so that her back was to Amberly. She whispered for a moment and then whirled back around and hung up the phone. "He's in his office. You can go on in."

Amberly walked through the gate that divided the public area from the more private space and headed directly to Cole's office. She knocked and heard his gruff response. She opened the door to find him seated behind his desk, a scowl doing nothing to detract from his handsomeness.

"I didn't expect to see you here today," he said.

"Why not? This is an active case and I intend to be here every day until you have the killer in jail." She closed the office door and took a seat in the chair across from him. "Granny Nightsong would take a look at your expression right now and say that the grouch bird bit you on your butt while you slept last night."

He stared at her in surprise. "And Granny Nightsong is..."

"My grandmother. She raised me from the time I was three until she died four years ago." She'd accomplished what she'd intended: his scowl was gone, at least for the moment.

"That's right, you mentioned her before."

"So, what have you learned since I left here yesterday?" she asked.

"I've been back to the crime scene to see if anything was missed but found nothing. There is a kill site somewhere, but we have no idea where it might be. My deputies have been pounding the streets interviewing Barbara's friends and family members. I've been going over the interviews as they bring them back to me."

"Anything specific jump out at you?" she asked.

He shook his head and leaned back in his black leather chair. "Nothing. It's just like the other two. Method of death was five stab wounds to the chest. According to the coroner who did the autopsy last night, the wounds were made with a six-inch straight blade and were in a downward motion, indicating that the killer was taller than the victims."

"Probably male," she replied.

"That's definitely the path I'm pursuing. Not only is there a height difference that would indicate a male killer, but it also takes a tremendous amount of strength to stab a chest as deeply as these victims were stabbed. She also had Taser marks and was bound at her wrists and ankles at some point before her death."

"After studying the files, I have a few more thoughts to add to the mix," she said.

He sat forward. In the small office, she could smell the scent of his cologne, a pleasant woodsy scent that fired her feminine hormones. His eyes were the blue of still waters, deep and fathomless, and his intense stare made her slightly uncomfortable.

"First of all, the killer obviously wants attention. He makes no attempt to hide his kills but rather displays them in public places. If I were you, I'd try to control the information any media outlet is getting. He'll feed on anything that's about the murders."

"I'd already thought about that, but in this day and age, it's fairly difficult to control the flow of information about anything," he replied, his frown threatening to return.

"The usual profile is that he's probably between the ages of twenty-five and thirty-five. He's probably a Caucasian, although I'll admit I'm not ruling out that it could be somebody of Native American descent."

"Is that why you were chosen for this particular assignment?"

She looked at him in surprise. To be perfectly honest, she hadn't considered it before this moment. "Maybe," she admitted. "I suppose it makes sense that the director would utilize me if he thought there was any kind of Native American overtones to the crimes."

"But except for the dream catchers, there aren't any other overtones," he replied.

"At least none that we've initially seen so far," she replied and then smiled. "I try to keep all my options open this early in an investigation." She crossed a leg and leaned forward. "And tell me, Sheriff Cole, you aren't a local here, right?"

"What makes you think that?"

"Your investigative skills are too sharp, your reports

too well written for a man who's spent his entire career in a small town."

"I grew up here and then left to go to college in St. Louis. Once I graduated, I joined the police force there and within two years had worked myself to detective."

That made sense, and she patted herself on the back for recognizing that he was more than a small-town sheriff, that he'd had his real training on the mean streets of St. Louis. "So, what brought you back here?" she asked, curious.

His blue eyes deepened in hue, becoming the haunting color of midnight. "I was working a murder case, a triple homicide. The FBI had been called in for some assistance, and of course, once they got involved, they completely took over the case."

He hesitated a moment and drew in a long, deep breath. "For some reason, the killer focused in on me personally. He managed to kidnap my wife."

Although his words were delivered in a flat, emotionless tone, Amberly sensed a wealth of pain beneath the words, a pain too great for expression. She felt a tightening in her chest as she recognized his story probably didn't have a happy ending.

"The killer, Jeb Wilson, held her in an abandoned house for two days. We finally managed to find the place and had it surrounded. I had found a way in through a broken window in the basement, but the FBI refused to let me go in. They had decisions to make, red tape to cut or whatever, and so the rescue process was delayed by twenty minutes. When we finally got inside, my wife was dead, but her body was still warm. She'd been killed within minutes of us getting inside. As far as I'm concerned, the FBI was as responsible for her death as Jeb Wilson."

DESPITE THE FACT THAT EIGHT long years had passed, the agony of that moment, of finding his wife dead, had never eased, had never lessened. And there had always been a part of him that blamed the FBI agents for not having the capability of moving fast enough when his wife's life had hung in the balance.

"I'm so sorry," she said, obviously aware that her words of consolation meant nothing. "You know, we don't always get it right."

Surprisingly, these words, the knowledge that she knew the agency she worked for sometimes screwed up, somewhat satisfied him. "Well, I don't intend to screw up these cases," he said. "The families of these women have a right to know what happened to them and why."

"The why isn't obvious yet," she said, a tiny frown dancing across the center of her forehead. "I'd like to see the reports and interviews your deputies have gathered together since I left last night. We need to somehow find a common denominator among these women. That would be the first step in identifying a possible motive and suspect. And we need to do it fast. There were four weeks between his first kill and his second and only two weeks between the second and third. We have no idea how quickly his time line is escalating."

"Don't remind me," he said dryly. He got up from his desk, finding the small office stifling with her scent wafting in the air and her presence far too close to his desk.

"Why don't we move to the conference room? Would you like a cup of coffee?"

"Absolutely. My belief is you can't have enough coffee, and you can't have enough red licorice." He looked at her in surprise. "Changed the nicotine habit to a licorice habit years ago and have yet to kick the licorice addiction."

"Personally, I'm a black-licorice kind of guy," he replied, as if he needed to remind her, assure himself of how different they were.

They stepped out of his office, and as she headed down the hall to the conference room, he went into a break room that held a round table, a minifridge and a coffeepot.

As he poured the coffee into two foam cups, an edge of irritation swept through him. He'd told her too much about himself. He didn't want her to know his personal information, and he certainly didn't want to know hers, but he'd spilled his guts to her, and he wasn't sure why.

He had three murders to solve, and he couldn't allow his head to get muddied with the evocative scent of her, the intelligent depths of her beautiful eyes.

She had a family, she was here to help him solve murders and not to awaken feelings that had been dead for eight years, feelings he never wanted to experience again.

By the time he walked into the conference room, he felt as if he was once again under control. He placed a cup of coffee in front of her at the table. "I wasn't sure how you liked it, so I brought some sugar packets along."

"Black is fine," she replied. "Did you know the victims personally?"

He took the chair next to hers so they were both looking at the bulletin board. "Mystic Lake is a small town. I know most everyone here personally."

"Tell me about the victims, information that wasn't in the official reports. What kind of women were they? What did they like to do in their spare time?"

He knew what she was attempting to do—she was hoping to find a connection between the three women, a connection that might lead them to the killer, a connection he had yet to make.

"First victim, Gretchen Johnson, worked as a bartender at a place at the edge of town called Bledsoe's. She was tough, had been around the block a few times and lived in an apartment behind the bar. Mary Mathis was a hairdresser at the beauty shop, lived at home with her parents and was dating Craig Brown at the time of her death," he began. "She liked to gossip, loved to shop and seemed well liked by everyone."

"Either of the other two victims go to that beauty shop?" she asked.

"According to the owner of the salon, neither Gretchen nor Barbara got their hair done there."

"So, we can mark that off as a potential connection for the victims."

He nodded, wishing he'd chosen the other side of the table to sit, where he wouldn't be so close to her. She wore no wedding ring, although he supposed there were plenty of married women around who didn't wear a ring.

He frowned and refocused. "I've tried to connect their lives, but these three women didn't know each other well. They didn't socialize together, they weren't involved in the same activities and hobbies. Mary was a chatty hair-dresser, Barbara was a shy teacher's aide and Gretchen was a bartender at a rough-and-tumble place on the north edge of town. I can't find where their lives intersected."

"If these are just random victims, then it's going to make our job that much more difficult," she replied as she stared at the board.

*Our job.*

She'd already taken half possession of the crime. He tried to be angry about it, but the truth of the matter was he wanted this killer caught before he killed again, and if it took Agent Amberly Nightsong's help to accomplish that, then he'd accept it. The stakes were too high to get into a territorial dispute.

"They might be random, but they have their approximate ages in common. However, Mary had light brown hair, Gretchen was dark haired and, as you know, Barbara was a blonde. So, at this point, we don't know that he has a specific type of woman, other than that they were all around the same age."

She pulled her braid over the front of her shoulder and toyed with the end of it, a gesture he found ridiculously sensual, as he could imagine the spill of that thick, shiny hair across his bare chest.

He jumped out of his chair, nearly upending his cup of coffee in the process. "I need to get out on the streets and check in with some of the townspeople. You're welcome to stay in here as long as you want."

"I'd much prefer to go with you," she said as she also rose from the table. She grabbed her purse, pulled the strap over her shoulder and then looked at him expectantly.

He'd be a total tool to insist she stay here. Besides, he had to stop fighting the fact that, at least for now, she was part of his team.

"Suit yourself," he replied. "I usually walk Main Street about this time of day. It's more important than ever this morning. Everyone will want to give me their take on the murder, and somewhere in the minutia of their gossip, I might glean a clue."

"Sounds like a plan," she agreed. "And maybe by the time we get back here, your deputies will have some more interviews for us to go over."

"I've got a meeting set up with everyone at one this afternoon so we can sort through all the information that's been gathered," he replied.

They stepped out into the bright morning sunshine, and Cole felt the tension that had ridden his shoulders since she'd first walked into his office finally begin to ease.

He'd worked most of the night, making notification to Barbara's family, seeking out potential witnesses and then studying the photos that had been taken at the scene.

Maybe it was because he was tired that he seemed so acutely aware of Amberly, not just as an FBI agent but as a beautiful woman. As he drew in a lungful of fresh air, he centered himself, pulling his mind from her and instead focusing on connecting with the people he served and trying to gain any information that might help him catch the killer who had struck not just once, but three times.

The sheriff's office was located smack-dab in the middle of the main drag of the small town. It was just before ten o'clock, and the stores were preparing to open.

He'd come back to Mystic Lake to escape his pain, and he'd found a home among good people who seemed to genuinely care about each other.

"It's a nice town," she observed after they'd walked a little ways.

"You hadn't been here before yesterday?" he asked.

"Never, although I've heard about the cool antique and craft shops. Some of my friends have gotten terrific stuff from here at great prices."

"And you aren't an antique bargain hunter?" He slid her a quick sideways glance.

"It seems like for the last four years I've been putting together a house where the most important room's décor has gone from dinosaurs to stars and planets and now to all things law enforcement. My living room is still half-done, my bedroom has nothing more than a bed and a dresser, but Max has the room that every six-year-old boy dreams about."

"What about your husband?" He couldn't help himself. He had to ask.

"Ex-husband. John is an artist. He does quite well painting Western pictures that sell for obscene amounts of money. He lives close to me, and we've remained friends, hoping that the divorce won't leave too many scars on Max."

"John Merriweather?"

She looked at him in surprise. "You know his work?"

He nodded. "I like his work. I just can't afford it." He

paused as Bill Walton, who owned an old-fashioned bar-bershop, stepped outside his shop's door and motioned to him.

"'Morning, Bill," he said to the thin, middle-aged man with a glorious mane of golden hair.

"Sheriff… Ma'am." His gaze lingered a moment on Amberly and then snapped back to Cole.

"Heard about Barbara Tillman. You got a suspect in these murders yet?"

"Yeah, and you're right on the top of the list," Cole said wryly.

Bill snorted. "Right. As if Erin would ever let me out at night to wander around for anything, and I guess by your answer that you don't have anyone on the suspect list." His gaze slid back to Amberly. "I don't believe we've met." He held out his hand. "Bill Walton, the one and only barber in town."

"Amberly Nightsong," she replied as she shook his hand and then released it.

"Amberly is with the FBI. She's helping me with the case," Cole said.

"Lucky you," Bill exclaimed. "Getting to hang around with a gorgeous woman all day. All I get is old men with hairy heads and ears."

Amberly smiled. "I'm just here to help Sheriff Cald-well solve the crimes."

Cole noted that her cheeks held a heightened color as if the compliment had embarrassed her. That single fact made her more human, and he felt a bit more of the ten-sion around his shoulders slip away.

They moved on from the barbershop, talking to people

and shopkeepers they met along the way. The topic of conversation was always the murder the night before.

Cole listened to their impressions and theories about the murders—and everyone had their own theory.

By the time they'd finished their walk down Main, it was close to noon. "I usually eat lunch at the café," he said and pointed down the street to a red awning. "Want to join me?"

"Sure. To be honest, I'm running strictly on coffee this morning and could definitely use something more substantial."

Within minutes, they were seated at a booth in the busy café, waiting for their orders to arrive. "I especially like the theory that it is space aliens coming into town to commit the murders and hang the dream catchers," she said, repeating what Wilma Townsend had said as they'd stopped at her craft store.

Cole smiled. "Every town has a resident kook, and Wilma is ours." His smile lasted only a moment. "What bothers me is that it's possible we spoke to the killer this morning, that he greeted us with a smile on his face."

"It's also possible he isn't a local," she replied. "You get a lot of transient traffic through town because of the unique shops and restaurants." He tried not to notice how the sunshine drifting through the window caught and gleamed on her hair. "We often find that the first victim holds most of the clues as to what drives the perp. You mentioned that Gretchen Johnson had a boyfriend?"

"Jeff Maynard. A hothead with a nasty reputation. They worked together at the bar, and the night of Gretchen's death, had a public fight before leaving work. I was so sure he was my man, but several of his friends swear that they all left work together and played poker until near dawn."

"Are these men who would lie for him?"

"Absolutely, but I haven't been able to break one of them. Then when Mary showed up dead, I couldn't find any connection between her and Jeff Maynard."

She frowned thoughtfully and took a sip of her water. As she placed the glass down, her gaze met and captured his. He'd never been a fan of brown eyes before, but hers seemed to draw him in. "Is it possible Jeff killed Gretchen, and then feeling the heat of your investigation and being your main suspect, he killed the other two to take the heat off him?"

Cole shrugged. "I suppose anything is possible at this point."

"I'd like to talk to Jeff. Can you make that happen?"

"Jeff kind of drifts during the week. He spends time staying at different friends' places, both here and in Kansas City. The best time to catch up with him is on a Friday or Saturday night at Bledsoe's, the bar where he works."

"Tomorrow is Friday. I'll plan on heading to the bar around ten. In my experience, nothing much happens before that time in bars."

"Why don't you meet me at my house and we'll go together?" he suggested.

"That isn't necessary," she protested.

"Oh, but it is. A beautiful woman like you would be eaten alive in that dive."

She leaned forward and gave him a smile that torched

through him. "Have you forgotten, Sheriff Caldwell, I'm an FBI agent and I carry a gun?"

"And might I remind you that you don't know the players, you won't know who else in the bar might be carrying, and as a responsible member of the law enforcement of this town, I can't allow you to go in there alone." There was more than a hint of steel in his deep voice.

He had no idea what the hell he was doing. He hadn't wanted her here in the first place, he didn't like the way she made him feel, and yet here he was, insisting he go with her to a rowdy bar on a Friday night.

He told himself he'd use her to help solve the crime and that was all he wanted from her, but even as this thought shot through his mind, it battled with the question of what her lips would feel like beneath his own.

# Chapter Three

Amberly managed to make it to John's house by four-thirty that afternoon to pick up Max. Earlier in the day, she and Cole had met with his deputies and compared notes.

Unfortunately, no information that the deputies had gathered had made for any kind of an aha moment. She was used to the cases she worked not being easily solved; what she wasn't used to was being so ridiculously attracted to a man she was working with.

She was a strong, independent woman, and yet there was something about the broadness of his shoulders that tempted her to lean against him. He had strong features and a square chin that she suspected held more than his share of stubbornness. But his lower lip was full and whispered of sexiness, and the blue of his eyes made her want to lose herself in them forever.

Still, no matter how attracted she was to him, she certainly didn't intend to follow through on it. She'd made a personal commitment not to date until Max was older. The relationship she shared with John was healthy and good, and Max had adjusted to the divorce very well.

He'd been so young when it had happened she doubted

that he even had any memories of her and John together. But she didn't want to screw anything up by introducing a new man to the mix, especially a man who might not be in her life, in Max's life, for the long haul.

If she ever decided to move on, whoever she did eventually invite into her life would have to be a very special kind of man. Max didn't need a father; he already had one of those. Any man who wound up in her life would have to understand that his role to Max would be as friend and confidante, a stepfather who had to work with John as the father.

It all felt so complicated, too complicated. And she wasn't the type for a random hookup. Although there were certainly times when Max was in bed asleep and Amberly missed having somebody there to talk to, to share the details of her day with, somebody who would hold her through the nights of both good dreams and bad.

Ultimately, the truth of the matter was that she didn't believe in the state of marriage. She didn't believe that passion could last for years, that the kinds of compromise that had to be made to make a marriage work was worth the benefit in the end.

As she pulled into John's driveway she noticed Ed Gershner's car parked along the curb. Ed was her next-door neighbor, a man in his mid-fifties who loved gardening, fine art and chess. He and the younger John had met at a community center where several people had been trying to form a chess club. The club hadn't happened, but a friendship based on the love of the game had formed between John and Ed.

Max greeted her at the door with a hug and a kiss and

then led her into the kitchen, where Ed and John were in the middle of a match.

Neither man looked up from the board. "Two minutes," John said. Amberly exchanged a grin with her son. They both knew the routine, that it was taboo to interrupt an active chess game.

She gestured her son back into the living room and pulled him down on the sofa next to her. By the time Max had finished telling her about his day in school, Ed and John joined them.

"He beat me again," Ed exclaimed in disgust as he raked a hand through his salt-and-pepper hair. "That makes twice this afternoon."

Amberly gave him a smile. "You'll get him next time." She looked at John. "I can take Max home tonight, but would you mind keeping him for the weekend?"

"You know I don't mind," John said.

"That okay with you, Max?"

"Sure. We can finish that puzzle we started," he said to his father.

John laughed. "I hate to tell you this, buddy, but I think it's going to take us longer than one weekend to get that sucker put together." He looked at Amberly with a woeful smile. "It's Buckingham Palace in 3-D."

"Whoa, sounds like a big job," Amberly exclaimed as she rose from the sofa. "Come on, Max. We'd better get out of here. I see Ed is chomping at the bit to have another game with your dad."

"And this time I'm going to get him," Ed vowed.

Max grabbed his backpack and ran over to give John a kiss. "Guess I'll see you tomorrow."

"I'll bring him after dinner," Amberly said. She didn't intend to go back to Mystic Lake until tomorrow night, when she was meeting Cole to go to the bar. She planned on spending much of the day comparing the files of the murders and the latest information and interviews that had been done during the last twenty-four hours and, of course, hanging out with her son.

As usual, as they drove the three blocks from John's house to theirs, Max insisted they play their game. He described in minute detail the front yard of a house they passed. He noticed a basketball half-hidden in the bushes, a red-and-white bicycle against the beige house and a patch of dry grass beneath a large pine tree.

"Awesome, Max," she exclaimed when he'd finished.

"You have to be good at that kind of stuff if you want to be an FBI agent, don't you, Mom?"

"That's right, but you also have to get good grades and make good choices when you're growing up. But you know, Max, you don't have to be an FBI agent. You're so smart you can be anything you want to be if you work for it."

"I know, but I want to be an FBI agent like you," he replied.

By that time, they had arrived at their house. Max went into his bedroom to play one of his video games while Amberly started frying burgers for dinner.

As she worked, she couldn't help it that her mind went back to Cole Caldwell. She'd gotten mixed messages from him all afternoon. There had been moments when she'd caught him staring at her, when she'd felt the heat of male interest emanating toward her. But they were brief moments followed by coldness and an edge of resentment.

She told herself she didn't care how he treated her, what his thoughts were of her. All that mattered was that they somehow figure out how to work together to discover who was killing the young women in Mystic Lake.

As she flipped the burgers and then made a quick salad, her thoughts moved from Cole to the crime. The dream catchers confused her.

It was a dichotomy for the killer to brutally stab three women to death and then hang a dream catcher above each victim as if to assure them happy dreams throughout eternity. What did it mean? What did the dream catchers mean to the killer?

After dinner, several games of Go Fish and a bath for Max, she tucked him into his bed for the night. "I'm sorry I won't be around this weekend," she said as she touched the owl pendent hanging around his neck.

"It's okay. Me and Dad will have fun. We always do. Now, tell me a Granny Nightsong story before I go to sleep."

"Granny Nightsong thought the wind was an old man who, when grouchy, blew. On a windy day, she'd yell at the old man, telling him to hush his mouth, to stuff a sock in it." Max giggled at this, and the sound wrapped around her heart and squeezed it tight.

"She was funny."

"She was funny and wonderful, and I wish she would have lived long enough that you could have grown up with her. She would have loved you so much."

Max nodded, his eyelids beginning to droop. "Are you working on an important job now?"

"Very important. I'm helping a sheriff find a bad guy. His name is Sheriff Cole Caldwell."

"Sheriff Cole… If I don't be an FBI agent, maybe I'll be a sheriff." His eyes drifted closed and she knew he was asleep. Still, she remained seated on the edge of his bed, drawing in the scent of childhood, of little boy… that scent that belonged to Max alone.

She and John might have gotten a lot of things wrong between them, but Max had been nothing but right. He was her heart, her hopes and dreams.

She finally got up from his bed and left his room. She went into the kitchen, poured herself a cup of coffee, threw a bag of red licorice on the table and then began to spread out the crime files.

There was no question that she was looking forward to tomorrow night and meeting up with Jeff Maynard and some of his friends at Bledsoe's. Amberly had good instincts about people, and they might be more apt to talk to a woman than to a sheriff.

Going back to the first murder of Gretchen Johnson made sense to her. That was where the killer established his pattern, that's where a possible personal connection could be found between killer and victim.

Cole had surprised her with his assertion that he go with her to the bar. There had been times during the afternoon that she'd thought he wanted her anywhere else but close to him.

He could go with her tomorrow night if it made him feel better, but that didn't mean they were going to stay together inside the place. She couldn't accomplish what she needed to with him at her side.

Although the idea of having him right at her side was far too appealing, she had to keep her personal, crazy attraction to him firmly under control.

She'd noticed as they'd walked the streets of Mystic Lake that morning that he was well liked and respected by the people he served. He probably had some hot honey-bunny at home to snuggle with, to get him through the long, lonely nights.

He'd told her his wife had been killed eight years before. Men didn't do well alone, and she couldn't imagine that a man like Cole Caldwell had spent the past eight years entirely alone.

Besides, she didn't care. She had a crime to solve, a son to raise, and that was more than enough for her at this time in her life. She'd stopped believing in long-term relationships and marriages when she'd finally decided to leave John. Whatever she felt toward Cole Caldwell was nothing more than a healthy dose of lust—and she had learned the hard way that friendships might last forever, but passion was a fleeting emotion meant to make fools of people.

AT PRECISELY NINE-THIRTY Friday night, Cole's doorbell rang. He'd expected her to be exactly on time, and she was. They'd agreed to meet at his house half an hour before leaving for Bledsoe's.

He opened the door to greet her, and for a moment, his breath caught in his chest. Clad in a pair of tight jeans and a turquoise, sparkly blouse, with her hair loose and flowing down her shoulders and back, she looked sizzling hot and definitely not like the professional agent he'd spent time with the day before.

He had foregone his uniform, opting instead for a pair of blue jeans and a short-sleeved button-down navy shirt. For an awkward moment, they simply stared at each other, and then he found his voice.

"Come in," he said as he gestured her inside. As she swept past him, her perfume teased his nose, and he felt a tightening of every muscle in his body.

"Nice place," she said as she entered his living room. "Very functional and masculine."

He looked around the room as if seeing it through her eyes. Functional, yes, but also cold and impersonal. When he'd bought this house and moved here, he'd still been reeling with grief. He'd bought the furniture he needed to exist, and that was it.

Since that time, he'd done little to make it a real home. It was just the space where he ate, showered and slept when he wasn't on the job.

He motioned her into the kitchen and to the small, round table. "Want something to drink?" he asked, wanting some sort of activity to take his mind off her sexiness.

"No, thanks. I figure I'll order something when we get to Bledsoe's," she replied as she took a seat at the table.

He remained leaning against the refrigerator, feeling the safety of that much distance from her. He'd noticed she was pretty the first moment she'd arrived at the scene. But it was as if on that day, she'd been a photo negative, and now she was a full-blown colored photograph.

"So, what's the plan?" he asked, since this was her idea to begin with.

"If things were going to go my way, then you'd stay here and I'd go to Bledsoe's alone."

He raised a brow and gave her a tight grin. "But you don't always get your way in life." The smile fell. "Bledsoe's is usually filled with a pretty tough crowd, all the lowlifes in town seem to gather there on the weekends. You aren't going in there alone."

"I'm also not going in there as an FBI agent asking questions," she replied.

He couldn't help the way his gaze slid down the length of her. "I'd say that's obvious," he replied dryly.

"So, we need to come up with a cover story of sorts if you're going to be with me. And by the way, I don't want you lurking at my side every minute of the night. That defeats everything I'm trying to do."

"I'll find some corner to sit in and nurse a beer," he replied.

"Have you done that before?"

"Occasionally but not often. When I have spare time in my life, I like to take my fishing pole and sit on the bank of Mystic Lake."

"There're fish in it?"

"Rumor has it that it was stocked years ago, but I've never caught anything. I just enjoy sitting alone to unwind after a long day."

"No girlfriend to help you unwind?" she asked.

"Nope. I have no desire for a girlfriend, a second wife

or a relationship. I'm satisfied with my work and my fishing time. That's enough for me." His voice took on an unintended rough edge. Never again would he put his heart on the line, never again would he risk going through the agony he'd experienced when he'd lost his wife.

"Okay. So, the plan," she continued. "I think we should tell anyone who asks that I'm an old friend who finally decided to come to town for a visit, and I insisted we go to the bar because you're kind of a fuddy-duddy and I'm a party girl."

"I'm not a fuddy-duddy," he said irritably.

"It's just a cover story," she replied with a small laugh. "I'm not actually accusing you of being a fuddy-duddy."

Still, there was something in her tone of voice, a wicked gleam in her dark eyes that made him suspect she might see him as a rigid, humorless man. That wasn't who he was…although perhaps that was the man he'd become over the past eight years. He shoved this troubling thought aside.

"Okay, so we have your cover. You're an old friend from St. Louis who has come to visit and insisted we hit the town's hot spot for the night." He shoved himself off the refrigerator as she got up from the table.

As she stood, he once again recognized how gorgeous she looked. She'd be eaten alive by the bozos in the bar, but maybe in that process, she'd be able to gain information that would lead to them catching a killer.

That's all he wanted from her, that's all he wanted at all. To get this killer off the streets before he struck again, and there was no question that he would strike again—it was just a matter of time.

Within minutes, they were in his car and headed to Bledsoe's. Cole believed the bar was a blight on the community, and more than once he'd been called there to break up a fight, to get a belligerent drunk home safely or disarm a drunk who had suddenly become a tough guy.

There was no question that it was a place where gossip was rife, where small stories grew to mammoth proportions, but there was also no question in his mind that Amberly might be able to learn more about the crimes than he had.

Nobody wanted to talk to a sheriff, but every man in the place, married or not, would want to find a way to talk to her, and hopefully one of them would be a little drunk and tell her a little too much.

"I feel like I'm putting you out there as bait," he said to break the awkward silence that had grown in the car as they drove.

She flashed him a quick smile. "Let's just hope I have more success at fishing than you usually do."

"Ah, low blow," he exclaimed.

"Granny Nightsong used to say that any fish could be caught if you just used the right bait. Of course, she also had a fish-catching dance that was an awesome thing to see."

Cole felt himself relaxing slightly. "She must have been a character."

"Oh, she was. I always like to describe her as full Cherokee and part crazy. She was the most important person in my life."

"What about your parents?"

"My father disappeared after impregnating my mother, and my mother was a crack addict who dropped me off at my granny's place when I was three. I never saw her again. I figure she's either dead or in prison." She said the words as if she'd long ago made peace with the facts of her life.

"You never tried to look for them? Your mother and father?"

She looked at him in surprise. "Why would I? They mean absolutely nothing to me. The best gift my mother could have given me was leaving me with Granny Nightsong and staying out of my life. I had a wonderful childhood with a woman who was strong and loving and just enough off center to be fun and exciting."

By that time, they had arrived at Bledsoe's. The bar was housed in a low, flat building with blinking beer signs at every window. The parking lot was full of pickup trucks, a few rusted old cars and several motorcycles.

"Wow, not exactly uptown, are we?" she muttered as they got out of the car.

Next to the bar was an old, abandoned warehouse with broken windows and a gaping front door. Cole had suspected for some months that drug activity took place in the building, but he'd never managed to catch anyone using inside, although he'd often found drug paraphernalia.

"This is an area of town I'd definitely like to see torn down and revitalized, but several of the town council members have interests in keeping Bledsoe's here."

As they approached the front door of the bar, the

sound of loud music spilled out along with the scents of booze, sweat and cheap cologne and perfume.

Instinctively, he grabbed Amberly by the elbow as they entered, as if subtly marking his territory to anyone who might see them.

She pulled away from him and beelined toward the bar, obviously not wanting him anywhere near her as she worked the room.

He found a small table in the corner and sat. From this vantage point, he could see Amberly wherever she went unless she disappeared into the back room, where there were three pool tables.

His stomach tightened as she sidled up to the bar and ordered a drink from Jeff Maynard. It was obvious she was flirting with him, and he was responding with more than a little bit of enthusiasm. At the same time, men moved in to flank each side of Amberly.

Cole knew the men. One was Raymond Ross, a single male with a reputation for being a ladies' man. The other one was Jimmy Tanner, a married man on the verge of divorce, according to local rumors. Both were good friends of Jeff's and had professed to being with him at the poker game the night of Gretchen's murder.

If Amberly was going to get any information, she was standing in the right place at the right time. Still, as he watched Raymond lightly touch her on the small of her back, Cole wanted to jump out of his chair and tell Raymond to keep his filthy hands to himself.

At that moment, Karen Kingman sauntered up to his table. Karen was well over fifty years old, and her face held the ravages of hard living, but she acted as if she was twenty-one and highly desirable.

"Hey, Sheriff." She batted her brown eyes. "As always, it's good to see you." She stood too close to him, invading his personal space as she leaned forward enough to flash him a view of her sagging, ample breasts. "What can I get for you?"

There was no question that she was hoping he'd say an order of her to go, but he ordered a bottle of beer and breathed a grateful sigh as she moved away. He focused back on Amberly.

She was now surrounded by half a dozen men, all obviously vying for her attention, and she appeared to be enjoying every minute of it. As he watched her toss her hair and laugh and accept a shot of something from Jeff, a rich desire for her flamed inside him. Yeah…him and every other man in the place, he thought ruefully.

For the next two hours, Cole sat at his table, watching as Amberly downed one shot after another, danced with one man after another and appeared to get more and more drunk with each minute that passed.

And Cole found his anger rising with each of those minutes that passed. What the hell did she think she was doing? How could she be effective doing her job with all the shots she'd consumed?

Had she forgotten why they were here? What was at stake? She was here to try to get answers, and instead, she was accepting drinks, hips swaying to the music as men vied for her company on the dance floor. She was not only wasting his time, but she was making a mockery of what they were trying to do.

By midnight Cole had had enough. Her cheeks were flushed, her natural grace gone as she stumbled between Jeff at the bar and Raymond and Jimmy. This had been a huge mistake.

He obviously hadn't known her well enough to trust this insane idea of hers. Dammit, he should have never agreed to this crazy plan.

And now he needed to get her out of here before she fell flat on her face and passed out. He walked over to where she stood at the bar between Raymond and Jimmy.

He took her firmly by the arm. "I think it's time we call it a night?"

"Ah, come on, Sheriff, it's early yet," Raymond said, his voice slightly slurred.

Jimmy threw an arm over Cole's shoulder, obviously more inebriated than his friends. "Yeah, don't go yet. We like your friend." He gave an exaggerated wink to Amberly, who giggled like a schoolgirl.

Cole was disgusted with the lot of them, Amberly most of all. He tightened his grip on her arm. "Sorry, boys, I think she's had more than enough for one night."

"The fuddy-duddy says it's time to go," Amberly said in dismay as Cole tightened his jaw. "But maybe I can come back tomorrow night." She leaned heavily against Cole as if not quite sure she could stand on her own.

As he led her to the door, he once again mentally cursed himself for agreeing to this plan in the first place. But the last thing he'd expected was his undercover agent to get totally wasted.

He walked her to the passenger side of his car, her stumbling and giggling while he cursed beneath his breath. He should have done something sooner. When he'd seen all the shots being bought for her, he should have stepped in and halted the whole thing.

They reached the passenger door. He opened it, but instead of sliding in, she grinned up at him. "You think I'm drunk, don't you?"

"I think you're smashed," he replied, his jaw tightening again.

"Then I demand a Breathalyzer," she exclaimed. Before he could guess her intentions, she reached up, leaned forward and pressed her mouth to his.

He had no idea what she intended, wasn't sure if she even knew what she was doing, but her mouth was hot and tasted faintly of tequila, and as she opened her lips beneath his, he took the invitation and deepened the kiss with his tongue.

He wasn't sure who halted the fevered moment of insanity, him or her, but suddenly he was staring at her in stunned surprise.

"If you thought that would convince me that you're sober, you're definitely wrong," he said. She slid into the car, and he slammed the door harder than necessary.

As he walked around to the driver's side, he realized what made him angry now was the fact that drunk or sober, he wouldn't mind kissing her again.

# Chapter Four

Amberly had no idea what had possessed her to kiss him.

It certainly hadn't been any alcohol that he thought she'd consumed. He slid behind the steering wheel and started the engine.

"I'm not drunk," she said. "And I should be livid that you'd think I'd get wasted when on an assignment."

"I saw the shots you drank." His voice was terse as he pulled out of the parking lot.

"Wrong. You saw the shots that were bought for me. You saw me holding those shots. You didn't see me actually drinking them."

He flashed her a quick glance. "So, what happened to the shots?"

"Part of them went on the floor, some of them went into that ugly plant at the edge of the dance area and two of them went down the sink in the ladies' room."

She noticed his hands slowly unclenching from the steering wheel. "You're a very good actress," he finally said.

"That was my second career choice," she replied, relieved that his anger seemed to be ebbing.

"So, what about that Breathalyzer?" His voice held the faint edge of tension.

"A moment of insanity. All women are allowed them occasionally." She couldn't explain it. She didn't want to think about that brief kiss. His mouth had been hotter, hungrier than she'd expected, and she hadn't wanted the kiss to end.

Crazy.

Maybe she'd consumed a little more of the alcohol than she thought she had. It was the only explanation for her sudden desire to feel his lips against hers.

"Did you learn anything?" he asked.

She was grateful to think of something other than that moment when his mouth had been on hers. "A little. I'll trade you information for a cup of coffee at your place before I make the drive back to Kansas City."

"Sounds like a wise idea."

From his reply, she had a feeling he still thought she was a little bit inebriated. They didn't speak again until they pulled up into his driveway. He cut the engine and turned to look at her. "Are you used to having that much male attention when you go out?"

She smiled and shook her head. "I don't go out."

"Why not?" he asked in obvious surprise. "You're young and attractive and single."

"I'm not looking for a man in my life. I have my work and my son and that's enough. Marrying John was a mistake, and I tried to make it work for three years, but I'm not sure I believe in long-term relationships."

"That's all I believed in until Emily's murder." He abruptly got out of the car, and she wondered if he was sorry he'd shared any personal information about himself and his marriage to the woman he'd loved.

"So, why aren't you in another relationship?" she asked as she followed him to the front door.

"Just not interested," he replied. He unlocked the front door and ushered her in before him. He led her to the kitchen, where she sat at the table while he made the coffee.

She wanted to ask him about his marriage, wanted to know if the passion he'd felt for his wife when they had first married had carried through the years that they'd been together.

Amberly only had her marriage to John as a reference point for the state of united bliss, and by no stretch of imagination had she felt bliss in that relationship. But there was something in Cole's set features that forbade her to ask any more personal questions.

Besides, she wasn't here to learn about his private life. She was here to help him solve a crime and nothing more. She definitely shouldn't be remembering the feel of his lips against hers. It was a useless waste of energy.

It wasn't until they each had a cup of coffee in hand and he was seated across the table from her that he spoke again. "So, what, if anything, did you learn?"

"First of all, Raymond and Jimmy hated Gretchen with a passion. Both of them said she was a bitch who kept Jeff from spending time with his friends and controlled Jeff's every move."

She paused a moment to take a sip of the coffee and then continued, "The fight that happened on the night of Gretchen's murder wasn't just between Jeff and Gretchen.

Jimmy and Raymond were involved in the argument, as well."

"Interesting." Cole cupped his large hands around his coffee mug. "The story I got at the time was the fight was strictly between Gretchen and Jeff, which is what put Jeff on the top of my suspect list when she wound up murdered. Now it sounds like I should have been looking more closely at Raymond and Jimmy."

"I wasn't able to break the poker-game alibi, but my gut instinct says they're lying about their whereabouts at the time of Gretchen's murder. Unfortunately, we can't arrest any of them on a gut instinct."

She took another sip of her coffee and found herself almost lost in the depths of his blue eyes. "Did you find any connection between the three of them and any of the other victims?" he asked.

"No, but I think it's worth looking into. The three of them definitely have a group mentality among them."

"Surely you aren't suggesting that all three are guilty of these murders?"

She leaned back in her chair and frowned thoughtfully. "There was nothing in any of the autopsy reports to indicate that the women were killed by more than one person. The knife wounds were consistent with a single killer. But that doesn't mean that the others weren't present when these women were killed, that it isn't possible they were the cheerleaders, so to speak, for the person who actually accomplished the crime."

She shrugged. "It's just another theory to consider or toss."

"At this point I think we have to consider everything

and toss nothing," he replied. "I definitely need to explore any relationship that might have existed between Jimmy, Jeff and Raymond and the victims."

"But we can't get tunnel vision," she replied. "It's quite possible that none of those men had anything to do with the murders. It would be a mistake to focus all of our energy on them and not look elsewhere."

"I agree. I've set up a couple of appointments tomorrow to reinterview some of Barbara's friends. I'm hoping that they might be able to tell me things about what was going on in Barbara's life that her parents might not have known about, things they didn't think about the night that my deputies spoke to them."

"I'd like to be there with you when you speak to them," she replied.

"Surely you'd rather have your weekend with your son." He took a sip of his coffee and eyed her over the rim of the cup.

"Max is used to spending the weekends with his dad. I'm free all day tomorrow, and I can't think of anything I'd rather do or anyplace I'd rather be." She leaned forward. "Cole, the time line worries me. I feel like every minute that passes brings us closer to another dead woman."

"Don't worry, I feel the tick of a bomb about to explode, too," he said grimly. "And on that note, you should probably get home and both of us should get some sleep. The first interview in the morning is at nine and it's almost one-thirty now."

A wave of weariness struck her as she realized how

late it had become. "Thanks for the coffee," she said as she got up from the table.

"Are you okay to drive home?" he asked as he walked her to the front door.

She turned and smiled at him. "Still suspect I'm only pretending to be sober?"

"No, and I apologize for doubting your work ethic." He smiled, and it was the first time she thought she felt some warmth behind the gesture.

And that warmth swirled around in her stomach, instantly evoking the memory of that brief kiss they'd shared. "I forgive you," she said briskly. "And I'll meet you at your office at nine in the morning."

Before he could even tell her goodbye, she turned and headed for her car in his driveway. Once she was on the highway heading home, she grabbed a piece of licorice from her console and chomped it down to nothing, hoping the taste would banish *his* taste from her mouth.

It was just before two when she finally pulled into her driveway. She parked in the driveway and half stumbled with exhaustion to her front door.

She had just unlocked her door when she thought she heard a rustling noise coming from the right corner of her house, where a large shrub stood sentry.

There was no wind. She frowned, frozen for a moment. "Hello?" she called softly. "Is somebody there?"

She remained frozen for several long moments but didn't hear the sound again. She shoved her door open, deciding that it had probably been a figment of her exhausted mind.

All she wanted was a hot shower and bed. She felt like

she'd been pawed by creeps all night and was eager to wash the nasty scent of Bledsoe's and unwanted touches off her.

Minutes later, as she stood beneath a hot shower, it wasn't thoughts of the investigation or Bledsoe's that filled her mind. Thoughts of Cole Caldwell and that crazy kiss they'd shared was all she could think about.

In that brief taste of his mouth, she'd felt more passion spark inside her than in all the kisses she had ever shared with John. For that single moment, it had been wild, insane really, the desire that had erupted inside her for him.

And she thought he'd felt it, too. She'd seen the stunned look in his eyes when the kiss had ended. Was it simply shock that she'd initiated a kiss with him at all, or had it been shock from the force of the chemistry that had sparked between them?

She dunked her head under the water as if to wash away all thoughts of the hot, handsome sheriff. All he wanted from her was her expertise as a profiler, and all she wanted to do was solve this crime and get on with the next one.

She stepped out of the shower and wrapped a large bath towel around her body. Quickly brushing her hair, she then braided it down her back. It would take hours to blow-dry it, so she often went to bed with a wet braid, which dried through the night while she slept.

It was as she stepped into her bedroom that a shadow danced across her window. Her heart leaped into her throat. Somebody was outside of her house.

With the towel still wrapped firmly around her, she

picked up her purse and withdrew her gun and house keys and then headed for the front door.

Her heart pounded as she unlocked her door and stepped outside in the darkness of the night. Had one of the men from the bar followed her back here? She didn't know if it was fear or the coolness of the September night that danced chills up her spine.

She waited for her eyes to adjust to the darkness, then with her gun clutched tightly in her hand and ready for anything, she stepped off her front porch.

Moving to the area where she thought she'd heard the rustling noise when she'd first arrived home, she whirled around the corner of the house and breathed a quick sigh of relief as she saw nobody lurking in the shadows.

With caution, she made a trip all around the house and saw nothing, and by the time she reached her porch once again, she wondered if her imagination had played tricks on her.

She'd been wound up by the drinks, by Cole and the kiss she'd shared with him and by the heinous crimes they were investigating.

It was possible the shadow she'd thought she'd seen at her window had been nothing more than a stray beam of moonlight, a passing car light on the street beyond the house.

Still, she didn't completely relax even when she was back in her bedroom and dressed in her nightclothes. She kept her handgun on the nightstand within easy reach.

There was no question that Jeff, Jimmy and Raymond wouldn't be happy to learn that she was an FBI agent working the murders in their town. And they *would* learn the truth about who she was and be able to guess what she'd been doing in Bledsoe's tonight.

She just hoped none of them knew where she lived. She just hoped the shadow she'd thought she'd seen had been nothing more than her imagination. The last thing she wanted to do was invite a killer to her home.

"HAVE WE GOTTEN THE LOGS of calls from Barbara's cell phone carrier?" Cole asked Deputy Roger Black.

"Yesterday. I've pored over them but don't see anything odd. Calls to her parents and several teachers, but no calls to or from men in the last month," Roger said. "Same with her laptop. I checked email, her favorites and her history, and nothing rang a bell. She didn't seem to be into social networking much."

Cole frowned. "So, we know she wasn't lured to the kill location by a phone call or an email."

"Wish we knew where the kill location was," Deputy Ben Jamison said.

"You all have checked the empty buildings, warehouses and anyplace that might hide a murder site?" Cole asked even though he knew the answer.

They all paused as the door opened and Amberly walked in. Cole could tell in an instant that she'd had a bad night. She looked tired and slammed her purse on the old wooden conference table as if it had personally offended her.

"Your granny Nightsong would take one look at your face and say that the grouchy bug bit you in the middle of the night," he said.

"Not enough sleep. Not enough coffee," she replied,

but a hint of a smile played on her lips. "And it's bird, not bug."

"Whatever. I can't help you with the first thing, but I can definitely get you some caffeine."

"I would really appreciate it," she said, her features softening even more as she greeted each of the other deputies. "I got up too late this morning to have any before I left home, and I'm really not very civilized before I have a cup of coffee in the morning."

"Well, I definitely want you civilized. I'll be right back." Cole quickly assigned his deputies to their tasks for the day, and they left the room with him, leaving Amberly alone.

There was nothing of the hot, sexy woman of the night before this morning. Clad in a pair of black slacks and a gray button-down blouse, with her hair pulled back in a braid and her makeup minimal, she looked every ounce of a tired FBI agent.

He could identify with the tiredness. It had taken him forever to go to sleep the night before. Her idea of a Breathalyzer had kept him awake for far too long.

He wasn't sure what had surprised him most, the fact that she'd initiated the kiss or his visceral response to it. He'd reacted to it like a dehydrated man offered his first sip of water.

He'd also been shocked by the surge of jealousy that had risen up inside him as he'd watched the other men interact with her.

He'd lived the past eight years of his life like a monk, uninterested in sex, focused solely on keeping the people of this small town safe and training his deputies to be the best that they could be trained.

If he had spare time, he used it to seek peace by sitting on the bank of Mystic Lake and either dwelling in old memories of the love he'd once had or shoving away all thoughts of what he'd lost.

That kiss had reminded him of the warmth of a female body pressed tight against his, of the spill of full breasts into his palms. He'd remembered the warmth of sheets cocooned around him as he explored the curves of the woman next to him.

The kiss had reminded him of early-morning coffee conversations, of the need to rush home after a long day at work to be greeted by somebody who loved him. He'd remembered all he'd denied himself for the past eight years. He'd wanted to honor the memory of his wife for the rest of his life.

He was a thirty-five-year-old man and the kiss had told him that he wasn't hormonally dead; his hormones had just been in a coma. But now they were awake and fully raging, and he wasn't sure what to do about it.

One thing was certain. He had no intention of allowing his hormones to get involved with Amberly Nightsong. First and foremost, she was his coworker and any physical relationship would only make things awkward between them.

Besides, she didn't appear to be the casual-hookup kind of woman, and that's all any woman would ever be in his life. Emily had marked his heart forever, scarring it with her absence in a way that left no space for another.

His anger and guilt about the manner of her death

haunted him in the night. How close he'd been to saving her and, ultimately, how tragic that he'd been mere minutes too late.

Whatever had occurred between Amberly and her husband had apparently left her scarred enough for her to be not willing to try it again. She'd said she was satisfied with her work and with her son. But that kiss had whispered of a hunger perhaps she didn't realize she possessed.

He shook his head as if to mentally clear it as he carried two cups of coffee back into the conference room and found her where she usually sat, facing the bulletin board. She appeared completely engrossed in the photos and barely nodded as he set her coffee on the table in front of her.

"Who are we meeting with this morning?" she finally asked, turning those dark eyes to look at him.

"Jenna James. According to everyone I've spoken to, she was Barbara's best friend. When my deputy spoke to her the night of the murder, she was too distraught to be much help. We're meeting her at her apartment."

"Anything specific I need to know?" She took a sip of the coffee, and her eyes began to take on a sharper, clearer view, as if the single shot of caffeine had focused her.

"Jenna works at the school where Barbara worked, and they lived in the same apartment building. From what I've heard, they did almost everything together. If anything was going on in Barbara's life, Jenna should know about it."

"And hopefully by the time we leave Jenna's apartment, we'll know everything from who Barbara was dating to who she had a secret crush on."

"I hope so," he said. He frowned and took a sip from his cup of coffee. "We need a break somewhere from someplace or somebody."

"There was a moment last night when I thought maybe the break was going to come when my dead body was found sometime this morning."

He started and stared at her, his heart taking an uneven rhythm. "What are you talking about?"

She smiled ruefully. "I thought maybe one of the boys in the bar had followed me home last night. First I thought I heard a rustling noise in the bushes next to my house, and then after I'd showered, I thought I saw something, or rather somebody moving outside my bedroom window." Her tone was light as if it was no big deal.

"Did you call the police?" he asked, thinking it was a much bigger deal than she obviously did.

"No, I went outside with my gun and checked out the yard. There was nothing there and no sign that anyone had been out there."

His heart nearly stopped at the idea of her being alone in the dark, gun or no gun.

"I think my imagination just went a little wacky," she finished.

He narrowed his eyes. "Does that happen a lot?"

"Almost never," she admitted. "I'm definitely not the type to see evil men lurking in shadows or believe somebody is after me. Last night was an anomaly, an acceptance that these murders have gotten to me like none have for a long time."

"And why is that?" he asked. After all, she probably worked dozens of cases a year in her career—she'd have to be good at compartmentalizing emotions, distancing herself from the victims, or she wouldn't be as effective in the job.

She frowned. "I'm not sure. Maybe because the women aren't that much younger than me. Maybe it's the dream catchers that were left at the scene or the fact that we have absolutely no evidence and few leads to follow." She shrugged. "At any rate, I definitely took the case home with me last night and was as jumpy as a silly girl in a horror movie."

"Are you sure there was nobody there?" He should have recognized the potential issues of allowing her to go undercover, so to speak, the night before. What if somebody did follow her home from here? Found out where she lived and how she might be vulnerable. What if it was the killer?

"As sure as I can be." She finished the last of her coffee and stood. "And we'd better get out of here if we're going to meet Jenna on time."

Together they left the conference room and headed out to Cole's official car. An uneasiness continued to gnaw at him as he thought about her leaving Mystic Creek each night to head back to Kansas City.

"You have to make sure that you aren't followed from here when you head home each day," he said when they were in his car and driving toward the apartment complex where Jenna lived.

He never should have agreed to her scheme the night before. He should have realized that sooner or later the three men she'd been chatting up for details about the crimes would identify her as the enemy, and if one of them was their killer, then they might have placed a giant target on her back.

# Chapter Five

"I'll be careful," Amberly said, not liking the fact that he'd reminded her that a serial killer was working a mere twenty minutes from her home and it was possible she'd already interacted with him.

Would it be a coup for that killer to murder a Native American female and hang a dream catcher above her head? What if that Native American woman was also an FBI agent on the hunt for him? Would that really spark his sick obsession? She fought a sudden shiver that tried to work up her spine.

"Thanks for adding to my bank of potential nightmare material," she said dryly.

He flashed her a quick glance. "Working as an FBI profiler you must have quite a bank of nightmare stuff. I'm sure you've seen plenty of terrible things."

"I have," she agreed. "But probably no worse than what you saw when working as a cop in St. Louis."

"Why an FBI agent?" he asked as he maneuvered a corner on the outer belt of the highway.

"I always knew I wanted to be something in law enforcement, I just wasn't sure what. When I was in high school, a bunch of my girlfriends got together for a night of watching horror films. You know, Freddie Krueger and Jason movies. We spent half the night squealing like babies, but then we decided to watch *Silence of the Lambs*. I wanted to be Jodi Foster. That was the moment I knew I was going to be an FBI agent. What about you? What drove you into law enforcement?"

"My father was a cop and so was Emily's dad. That's how we met, through our parents. To be honest, it never really crossed my mind to be anything else but a cop."

"Are your mom and dad still alive?"

"Mom died of breast cancer when I was ten. Dad passed away from a heart attack two years after my marriage. I guess I should be grateful that neither of them were alive to see Emily murdered." His hands tightened on the steering wheel, and for just a moment, Amberly wanted to reach out to him, to somehow ease the pain that seemed to drive him through life.

"Granny Nightsong used to say that emotional pain that you can't let go of is kind of like having a tick in your armpit. You don't know it's there until it has sucked the last of everything good out of you," she said softly.

He flashed her a look of obvious irritation. "You asked me a question and I answered it. Nobody was talking about any emotional pain."

An uncomfortable silence reigned for the remainder of the drive to Jenna's apartment building. The building itself was a nice three-story, painted beige and with neatly manicured lawns. There was covered parking in one area of the lot and a larger uncovered area in another.

Cole pulled into a spot marked with a visitor sign and the two of them got out of the car. "Maybe it would be best if I do the talking," Amberly suggested and watched the tension of an additional irritation sweep over his handsome features.

"And why is that?" he asked.

"Because Jenna is a young woman, and she would probably respond better, woman to woman, to me than to you. Sometimes, you come across a little scary."

He frowned, and his eyes were narrowed slits of blue ice. She grinned at him. "You're doing it right now... looking scary," she exclaimed.

"Then why aren't you scared?" The frown eased, and the blue of his eyes warmed a bit.

"There's only one thing in this entire world that scares me, and that's if anything bad happened to my son, Max. He's the sun in my sky, the wind on my face—" She broke off, half-embarrassed by her fervent verbal expression of love.

For an instant, Cole's features softened and his eyes took on the warmth of a summer sky. "That's the way I felt about Emily. She was my sun, and since her death, the world has been nothing more than gray shadows." He straightened his shoulders, and that moment of softness in his features snapped away. "Enough of this, we have work to do."

She followed his long strides as he went to the main entrance of the building. A small lobby held two elevators, and he punched the up button. "Jenna lives in 203 and Barbara lived in 205."

"So, they were right across the hallway from each other?" she asked as they stepped on the elevator. He nodded affirmatively. "I'm assuming you traced back

Barbara's activities to find out exactly when and where she was taken?"

"Her car was found abandoned at a convenience store. Unfortunately, it was in an area where the security cameras caught nothing of what might have happened. They did have her on tape coming into the store to buy a loaf of bread at seven-thirty that evening, but she apparently never made it back to her car." The doors to the elevator opened, and he gestured her out.

It took them only a moment to locate unit 203 and Cole knocked on the door. Jenna James was a small woman with petite features. Her blond hair was short and wispy around her face, and she was so thin it looked as if a puff of Cole's breath could blow her right away.

"Jenna," he said with a surprising softness.

"Sheriff Caldwell." She nodded and opened her door wider to allow them both inside as Cole made the introductions between Jenna and Amberly.

The living room was nice-sized and decorated in contemporary fashion in shades of black and gray and splashes of bright orange. The coffee and end tables were glass, and it was obvious that either Jenna was a great housekeeper or she had gone to extra trouble to have the place pristine when they arrived.

Amberly moved one of the orange throw pillows aside as she and Cole sat side by side on the sofa and Jenna sank down in the modern-looking chair facing them. "I still can't believe she's gone," Jenna said, tears welling up in her green eyes. "Every morning when I wake up, my first instinct is to go across the hall to have coffee with her."

"She was a good friend," Amberly replied, not having to work hard to inject sympathy into her voice.

Jenna nodded her head. "She was the very best. We did everything together. She was like the sister I never had." The tears trekked down her cheeks, and she quickly swiped them away, but it was a futile process as more tears followed.

"What we want more than anything is to catch the person who murdered her, and anything you tell us about Barbara might help us," Amberly said.

She was vaguely surprised that Cole had taken her advice and was obviously taking a backseat to the questioning. Her respect for him grew the more time she spent with him.

"I want to help in any way I can," Jenna agreed. "I just don't know if I have any information that might be helpful."

Amberly smiled at her reassuringly. "You'd be surprised at what little tidbit of information might help us break the case. Tell me about Barbara, what kind of woman was she?"

"She was beautiful on the inside and out. She made people feel good." As Jenna spent the next fifteen minutes extolling all the virtues of her friend, Amberly thought she sensed a touch of impatience wafting off Cole.

But Amberly knew the only way to get to Barbara's secrets was through building a bit of trust between herself and Jenna. And there was no way to hurry it. Trust took time, and Cole would just have to be patient.

"Was Barbara seeing anyone?" Amberly asked when Jenna had finally run down and paused to take a breath.

"No. Both of us were kind of between relationships," Jenna replied.

"Who was the last person she was in a relationship with?" Cole asked as if unable to contain himself another minute.

"For about three months she dated Tom Courtland, the gym teacher at the school, but they broke up about six months ago."

"Was the breakup friendly, or contentious?" Amberly asked.

Jenna smiled sadly. "Nothing about Barbara was ever contentious. No, the breakup was friendly. They both decided they were better off as good friends. The romantic spark just wasn't there between them, and they were both on the same page when the end came."

How well Amberly could relate to that. It had been part of the story of her failed marriage. "So, she hadn't been with any other man since breaking up with Tom?"

Jenna's gaze shot to the left and down and then quickly met Amberly's once again. "Not that I can think of."

She was lying. She knew something more than what she'd told them. She was keeping a secret for her dead friend, and in that secret might be the information they needed.

Amberly leaned forward, holding Jenna's gaze intently. "Jenna, nothing you tell us now can hurt Barbara. No silly gossip, no little secrets can change the fact that she's dead and she won't have to face any consequences of a secret coming out."

Jenna's cheeks grew a dusty pink and once again she broke her gaze with Amberly. *Bingo,* Amberly thought. She was definitely holding something back.

Jenna released a tremulous sigh. "Barbara had a one-night stand a couple of weeks ago. It wasn't something she was proud of, and it was definitely something she'd never done before. If we hadn't drank so much that night at Bledsoe's, it would have never happened. She just really wasn't that kind of person."

"Who?" Cole asked. "Who did she sleep with?"

Jenna looked back at Amberly, a faint plea in her eyes. "Barbara was a good person, and she had high morals. It was all just a terrible mistake."

"We're not here to judge her. We just want to find out who killed her," Amberly replied softly.

Jenna drew a deep breath. "It was Jimmy. Jimmy Tanner. He told her he was in the midst of a divorce, and that night at the bar he kept buying her drinks and was being so flirty with her. She got a little drunk and ended up going with him that night to the motel. The next morning, she was horrified at what she'd done."

Amberly and Cole exchanged a quick glance. That placed Jimmy in contact with two of their victims. He'd just moved up on their very short suspect list.

"Did Jimmy want to continue things after that night?" Cole asked.

Jenna shook her head. "No, not at all. He and Barbara didn't even speak to each other after that night. But they didn't exactly run in the same crowd. Barbara worked at the school and spent most of her evenings with me, either eating out or watching old movies here in my apartment." Tears once again filled her eyes. "It was my idea to go to Bledsoe's that night. I'm the reason she hooked up with that lowlife." Once again, she swiped at her tears. "Do you think it was him? Do you think he killed her?"

"At this point, we're just gathering facts," Cole said. He rose from the sofa as if instinctively knowing that there was nothing more Jenna could offer them.

They left Jenna's and met with two more of Barbara's friends, a coworker at the school where she worked as a teacher's aide and the man she had dated for six months and then broken up with.

Tom Courtland told the same story Jenna had about his breakup with Barbara. The two had dated but realized their relationship was based on friendship rather than any real love interest. He had an alibi for the night of her murder, and Cole and Amberly left with the intention of checking it out.

Neither of the two people they spoke to appeared to know anything about the wild night Barbara had spent with Jimmy Tanner in a motel room.

It was almost one o'clock when they exited Tom Courtland's, and Deputy Black pulled up next to Cole's car. He got out of his vehicle, a grim expression on his face.

"Roger, what's up?"

"We've got another one." The words hung in the air, and for a moment Amberly couldn't even make sense of them. Another one? Another murder already?

"Who?" Cole asked, his tone terse and filled with the

same kind of dread that weighed heavy in Amberly's heart.

"Casey Richards."

"Where?" The word shot out of Cole like a bullet.

"He hid this one a little better than the others," Roger said. "She's in the back of the alley between the Dollar Store and Suzie's Collectibles. Looks like she was killed sometime during the night and she was stuffed between the two garbage bins."

"Is there a dream catcher there?" Amberly asked.

Roger nodded. "Same as the others. Looks like she was stabbed multiple times in the chest, and one of those dream catchers is hanging from a string and dangling over her head."

"We're on our way."

Both Cole and Amberly jumped in his car. Cole started the engine with a roar and then slammed his fists down on the steering wheel and cursed.

Amberly understood the anger that erupted inside him; she felt the same kind of rage along with more than a little bit of fear. It was the fear that they were no closer to catching the murderer and the knowledge that the time between his kills had shortened to almost nothing.

IT WAS AFTER ONE IN THE morning by the time the newest crime scene had been processed and everyone pertinent to the victim and the crime had been interviewed.

Cole and Amberly were the only ones remaining in the conference room, where the bulletin board now held the photos of Casey Richards taken at the scene of the dump sitc.

Cole's eyes felt gritty with exhaustion and the weight of frustration he'd carried all afternoon and evening. Amberly looked exhausted, as well. They'd had nothing to eat all day, their entire focus on the new victim and the agonizing realization that the killer was on a time line that they couldn't predict.

"We need to call it a night," he finally said, breaking the silence that had momentarily lingered between them.

She nodded. "You're right. I can't think anymore. My brain is completely fried."

He leaned back in the chair and studied her features. She was truly one of the most beautiful women he'd ever seen, but right now, she looked utterly drained, and the idea of her getting into her car and driving the twenty minutes home concerned him. It was already so late, and he hated the fact that on some level he was worried about her.

"I've got an extra bedroom at my house if you want to just crash there for the night instead of making the drive back to your place in Kansas City." He didn't really expect her to take him up on the offer, but she tilted her head to the side, looking thoughtful.

"Does the offer of a room come with an offer of any kind of food?" she asked.

He nodded. "I could probably whip up a couple of omelets and some toast."

"At the moment, that sounds like manna from heaven," she replied. "I vaguely remember a cup of coffee this morning, but we haven't fueled up since then. And to be honest, I am really too tired to make the drive home, but I could get a motel room for the rest of the night."

"Nonsense," he replied as he pulled himself up and out of his chair. "We'll eat and then you can crash in my spare room. It's not a big deal."

Half an hour later, they were in his kitchen. Amberly sat at the table, her eyes narrowed to tired slits as he stood at the stove, making a cheese-and-mushroom omelet for them to share.

He hadn't thought it would be a big deal, her being here in his kitchen, her sleeping in his spare room. But as he worked on the food, he was acutely conscious of the scent of her, which had lingered in his head all day long. He was far too aware of his desire to tangle his fingers into that glorious mane of hair and repeat the kiss they'd shared when they'd left Bledsoe's.

As he popped the bread into the toaster, he thought that it seemed like a lifetime ago that they had gone to the bar together and had shared that crazy kiss.

"Tell me about your son," he finally said, hoping that any discussion of a six-year-old boy would drive any inappropriate thoughts he might entertain right out of his mind.

The smile that swept over her features was so beautiful it nearly stole his breath away. "He's the most handsome, good-natured genius I've ever known," she replied.

He smiled. "Sounds like a true motherly description to me."

She swept her long braid back over her shoulder. "Okay, I'll admit it, I might be a little bit biased. But honestly, he is a good-looking kid and he's very easygoing and more than a little bit brilliant."

"What do six-year-olds do nowadays?" Cole asked as

he buttered the toast that had popped up. "Is he all into the video and computer stuff?"

"Actually, we've tried to keep that stuff away from him, but he has video games like every other kid his age. He and John spend a lot of time putting together puzzles and playing mind games. Max wants to be an FBI agent when he grows up, so he and I have a special game we play."

He placed the plates with the omelets and toast on the table and then sat across from her. "What kind of a game?"

She picked up her fork and cut into the omelet. "It's kind of a spin-off of the old I Spy game. Instead of me saying I spy something red or green and him trying to guess what it is, I point out a person or a place, give him a couple of seconds to look and then he can't look again, and he describes as many details as he can to me."

"And how does he do?"

She took a bite of the omelet and washed it down with a sip of milk before answering. "Better than a lot of other agents I've worked with in the past. He has a real attention to detail for somebody so young."

Cole had once wanted children. As only children, both he and Emily had had a desire to fill a house with babies. They had decided to wait a couple of years before starting their big family, and when they had finally decided to get pregnant, it hadn't happened.

"At the time of Emily's murder, I was grateful that she and I hadn't had any children to grieve for her, that there were no little ones depending on me for solace," he said thoughtfully. "But hearing you talk about your son makes me wish that Emily and I had had a child."

Amberly reached across the table and lightly touched the back of his hand, her eyes filled with a sympathy he both embraced and abhorred.

She pulled her hand away and instead picked up the last of her piece of toast. "Granny Nightsong would say that you're a man trapped in the valley of shadows and you don't realize that it's your choice whether you decide to climb out or stay there."

"I'm not sure I'd like your granny Nightsong," he said, knowing that the topic of conversation combined with his frustration and exhaustion had sparked a sharp edge of irritation inside him.

"Everyone loved Granny Nightsong," she countered, and there was a wistfulness in her voice that spoke of her own grief. "There isn't a day that goes by that I don't miss her." Her eyes suddenly welled up with tears and she quickly shoved back from the table. "I've got to go to bed. When I start getting emotional, I know I've passed the point of exhaustion and entered the land of maudlin."

She carried her plate to the sink, rinsed it and then placed it in the dishwasher. He did the same, and together they left the kitchen.

He led her to his guest bedroom, which contained nothing more than a bare dresser and a double-size bed covered in a light blue bedspread. "The bathroom is right across the hall. Anything you need, you should be able to find in the cabinets and towel closet."

"Could I bother you for one of your T-shirts to sleep in?" she asked.

The idea of her naked beneath one of his shirts shot a sizzle of heat through him. "I'm sure I can find something for you," he said and hurried down the hallway toward his own bedroom.

As he rummaged through his dresser drawers for a clean white T-shirt, he tried to keep Amberly out of his head. She was the first woman he'd invited into this home, but he reminded himself he'd made the invitation to her due to necessity. It was already almost two in the morning. He hadn't wanted her on the road at this time of night, driving while exhausted beyond reason.

By the time he got the shirt back to the guest bedroom Amberly was seated on the edge of the bed, running her fingers through her unbound hair.

Cole froze in the doorway. It was the sexiest thing he'd seen in years, and every muscle in his body tensed in response. "Here you go," he said as he tossed her the T-shirt. "Good night," he muttered and then raced back down the hallway to his own bedroom.

What in the hell was wrong with him? He placed his gun on his nightstand and tore off his clothes down to his boxers. He tossed his uniform into the hamper in his master bath and then crawled into bed.

Maybe this sexual attraction to Amberly was simply a way for him not to deal with the fact that he had a serial killer operating in his town. He had four dead women crying out for justice, and at this moment, all he could think about was Amberly's full bare breasts pressed against the cotton of his shirt, the long length of her legs beneath the hem.

He should be thinking about suspects and crime-scene reports, he should be putting together pieces of the puzzle that would solve these crimes.

But his brain was spinning with too much useless information, too many dead ends, and it was just so easy to think about Amberly as sleep slowly took over.

He awakened to an indistinct noise. Instantly, he grabbed his gun, jumped out of bed and hit the button on the lamp next to the bed that illuminated his room.

A glance at the clock let him know it was almost five. Predawn darkness still lingered outside the window. He heard the noise again and, this time, knew instantly what it was.

Amberly.

Apparently the dark dreams had found her tonight.

He set his gun back on the nightstand, turned on the hall light and lightly padded down the hallway toward her bedroom. As he drew nearer to her doorway the noise grew louder, a moaning of terror barely leashed.

Her door was open, and the spill of the light from the hallway splashed onto the bed. She was on her back, thrashing with the top sheet as if it had attacked her. Her hair was a dark tangle all around her head, half obscuring her lovely features, which were twisted in fear.

He remained frozen in place, unsure if he should pull her from the nightmare that obviously haunted her or allow the dream to come to its natural conclusion. Wasn't there some old wives' tale about waking somebody from a nightmare? Damned if he could remember what it was.

As a pitiful whimper escaped her lips, he realized he couldn't just stand by and allow her to suffer through whatever night terrors consumed her.

He walked to the side of the bed, and her exotic floral scent immediately assailed him. She'd told him she used her nightmares to get in touch with the kinds of evil that committed the crimes she investigated. Was she dreaming about the murders in Mystic Lake? Or were her nightmares from other murders, other towns?

As her moan became a louder cry, he reached out and gently touched her shoulder. "Amberly," he said softly. "Wake up."

She shot up to a sitting position, her eyes open and darting wildly around the room. When her gaze landed on him, she shuddered, then stilled and finally released a deep sigh.

"What time is it?" she asked, her voice slightly husky as if she'd been screaming in her dream.

"Just a little after five." He tried not to notice how sexy she looked in the T-shirt, how full her breasts were beneath the thin material.

"I'm sorry I woke you." She shoved the thick curtain of her hair behind her shoulders.

"Don't apologize."

"Was I screaming or slobbering or doing something totally embarrassing?" she asked.

He smiled. "None of the above, but you were making enough noise for me to know that you were having a nightmare. I wasn't sure if I should wake you or not."

She frowned. "I'm glad you did. I *was* having a nightmare. It's a recurring one that I have when I'm particularly stressed or tired." She pulled a strand of her hair back over her shoulder and played with the ends as if the motion somehow soothed her.

It didn't soothe Cole. It half hypnotized him, making his fingers itch to stroke the shiny richness of hair for her…for himself.

"I dream about Max. He's running in the dark and he's so afraid. I feel his fear so deep inside me." She took a fist and pressed it against her heart as if an intense pain resided there. "And I know he's lost his necklace and without it evil will find him."

"Necklace?" He tried to focus all his attention on her words.

She nodded. "It's a necklace my grandfather made for me when I was young, a protection charm of a silver owl he wears all the time. In the dream, it's gone and I can't get to him and I don't know what he's running from or what is keeping me from going to him."

He desperately wanted to stay focused on what she was saying, on the visions she'd told him had haunted her sleep, but his gaze kept wandering to the fullness of her breasts beneath his T-shirt, to the length of long, shapely bronze leg that had slipped out from beneath the sheet.

She must have sensed the direction of his thoughts, felt the tension that suddenly snapped in the air between them. It was five o'clock in the morning, she'd just had a horrible dream, and he wanted her more than he could ever remember wanting a woman.

Abruptly, she stopped talking, and her eyes darkened and yet sparked in their very depths with a shimmer that beckoned him. Her tongue slid across her bottom lip as if her mouth had become too dry or as if she anticipated the possibility of a kiss.

His feet moved him a step closer to the bed, and for

a moment their gazes remained locked together, a question hanging between them that he knew, in the logical part of his brain, was better left unasked.

She tossed the hair back over her shoulder once again and covered her bare leg with the sheet. "Thank you for waking me," she said as she broke eye contact with him and instead stared at the wall just behind him. "And now, we both better get back to sleep. Tomorrow is going to be another long day."

He thought he heard a touch of regret in her voice as his feet moved him back from the bed. "Absolutely, you're right," he said as he attempted to tamp down the desire that had hit him so forcefully in the gut. "Good night, Amberly."

As he left the room and headed for his own bedroom, he thought of that moment when the tension had sizzled in the air between them. She'd felt it. She'd wanted it. She'd wanted him.

He got into his own bed with the certainty that before this case was solved, he and Amberly were probably going to make a mistake, that they would wind up sharing a bed.

There was definitely something between them, an overawareness of each other that didn't just whisper of some underlying desire, but rather screamed it.

He had to remind himself that the last time he'd metaphorically gotten in bed with the FBI, there had been tragic consequences. He wasn't sure it was a good idea to really get into bed with with an FBI agent. Somehow, someway, he feared the consequences would be equally devastating.

## Chapter Six

It was four o'clock in the afternoon when Amberly decided to call it quits and head for home. She had arrived at the sheriff's office before seven that morning and had spent most of the day in the conference room. It had been a stressful day, first dealing with the details of the latest murder and second with the awkwardness that had somehow sprung up between her and Cole since they'd gotten up that morning.

"I'm going home," she said as she got up from the conference table where they had spent most of the afternoon. "I need to check in on my normal life and get away from all this for a few hours."

Cole rose, as well. "I don't blame you. You've definitely been putting in the overtime."

"So have you, and I know you won't be stopping work while I'm gone, but I'll be back in the morning, and you can catch me up."

Together they walked down the hallway and out the front door of the station house. "I'm sorry if I was initially an ass to you," he said, surprising her. "I appreciate your help and your insights into this case. I was just angry that the mayor decided to contact the FBI before he spoke to me about doing it."

"You and the mayor don't get along?" she asked.

"Mayor Justin Broadburn is an arrogant ass who thinks he's going to turn Mystic Lake and its quaint little shops into a desirable tourist trap."

"Murders aren't exactly conducive to bringing in tourists," she replied dryly.

"Exactly, and he's breathing down my neck like a fire-shooting dragon with every day that passes, with each new murder that's committed." He raked a hand through his thick, dark hair. "Get out of here. Go home and hug your son and do something normal for the rest of the evening."

She flashed him a smile. "That's exactly what I have in mind."

"Hey, Pocahontas." The deep voice came from somewhere in the distance.

Amberly tensed as she watched Jeff Maynard cross the street with long strides to approach her, a nasty twist to his features.

"Hi, Jeff," she replied, vaguely aware of Cole stepping closer to her as if anticipating trouble.

"Imagine my surprise when I found out the hot woman I partied with on Friday night was actually an FBI agent working murder cases and trying to pump me and my friends for information. You're quite beautiful and an accomplished liar, Agent Nightsong."

"I didn't lie about anything," Amberly countered.

"You didn't tell us you were an FBI agent," Jeff replied, his anger evident in the stiff set of his shoulders and the sneer that lifted his upper lip.

"You didn't ask," Amberly replied easily.

"But while you're here, I'd like to ask you some questions about your whereabouts last night," Cole said. He walked to Jeff and took him by his arm. "Why don't you come inside with me and we'll have a little chat."

Jeff jerked his arm away. "Maybe I don't feel like having a little chat right now."

Cole shrugged easily. "We can do it now and get it out of the way, or we can do it when it's a hell of a lot more inconvenient for you, but one way or the other, I need to interview you."

There was a glare-off between Cole and Jeff, and finally it was Jeff who broke the eye contact. "Whatever," he said. "Let's just get it over with."

As Cole led Jeff into the building, Amberly fought the impulse to follow behind them to see what Jeff might know about this latest murder, but she knew that Cole would do a good job, and Jeff might be more open if she wasn't in the room. He'd looked as if he'd wanted to tear her head off over her little game that night at Bledsoe's.

The best thing she could do was go home and spend the evening with Max. After the dream she'd had the night before, all she wanted to do was wrap her arms around her son and squeeze him half to death.

As she thought of that moment in the predawn hours when Cole had awakened her, a shiver slowly worked its way up her spine. The mutual desire between them had been obvious. His eyes had glinted with a silvery-blue light that had threatened to seduce her into inviting him into her bed.

She'd never felt such sexual longing for a man. Certainly not in her marriage to John and not since her divorce from him. It was a completely alien emotion for her, and she wasn't sure what to do about it. Ignore it? Pretend it didn't exist? Follow through on it?

Oh yes, she wanted to follow through on it. She wished she'd scooted over and raised up the sheet to allow him to join her in the bed last night.

To what end? She certainly wasn't looking for anything long-term in her life. She didn't even believe in long-term relationships. And Cole was at the opposite end of the pole, apparently content with the marriage he'd shared with his wife and unwilling to move forward from that.

But isn't that what made him a perfect candidate for a quick, meaningless hookup? Heck, half the time she wasn't even sure she liked Cole Caldwell, and the other half of the time she found herself imagining his strong arms around her, his mouth pressed tightly against her own.

As she drove, she glanced in her rearview mirror often, making sure she didn't see a car following her. She didn't want anyone from Mystic Lake following her home unless he was in the sheriff's car and his name was Cole Caldwell.

Jeez, this case was making her crazy in more ways than one. They'd spent the day trying to make connections between the newest victim and all the others. They'd tried to tie Jeff Maynard, Jimmy Tanner and Raymond Ross to all of the victims, but other than Jeff dating Gretchen and Jimmy having a one-night stand with Barbara, there was a lack of a real trail to follow.

She shoved thoughts of crime scenes and murder out of her head as she pulled into John's driveway. As she got out of the car, she smelled the odor of the brick charcoal grill coming from the backyard, and it evoked memories of when she and John had been married.

He'd always said he hated a gas grill and much preferred the smokiness of cooking out over hot coals. He'd built the barbecue pit himself and during the summers they'd often enjoyed time on the deck with some kind of meat filling the air with mouthwatering scents.

John answered her knock on the door. "Hey, you're just in time. I was about to put some burgers on the grill. Max is out on the deck. Why don't you let him stay to eat…? In fact, why don't you join us? I've got plenty."

"That's the best offer I've had all day," she replied with a smile.

She followed him through the living room and kitchen to the door that led out on the back deck. Max greeted her with a happy hug and then went back to standing at the barbecue pit, apparently taking his role as keeper of the tools very seriously.

"Dad, they're starting to turn gray," he said.

"Great, that means it's time to put the hamburger on," John replied.

"Is there anything I can do to help?" Amberly asked.

"Sure, if you want to set the table out here, that would be great."

For the next twenty minutes they fell into a comfortable routine. Amberly knew exactly which cabinet to go to for the bright green heavy-duty outdoors plates and utensils while John threw the burgers on the grill.

As the meat cooked, John got out potato salad and baked beans while Amberly grabbed the ketchup and mustard and a jar of dill pickles. Max added napkins to the table and then sat watching the burgers finish cooking.

Dinnertime was filled with good food and laughter as both Max and John were at their most charming and entertaining. Amberly felt the tension of the past couple of days slowly easing from her shoulders.

She ate like a truck driver who hadn't seen food for months and laughed as John and Max teased her about her appetite. "Your dad is right. There's nothing better than a charcoal-grilled burger," she exclaimed as she squirted mustard on her second one.

"With lots of pickles," Max agreed as he dug his fingers into the pickle jar. Amberly started to say something about manners but decided just to enjoy the moment of her son's mischievous grin and her ex-husband's laid-back attitude.

As they ate they talked about Max's school activities, John's painting and the art show he was planning to have next month.

John didn't ask any questions about Amberly's work, and she hadn't expected him to. Even though she'd been an FBI agent when they'd first met and later married, it had always been something he'd insisted she keep private.

When they were finished eating, Max asked if he

could play outside next door with a friend of his, and Amberly agreed so she could help John with the cleanup.

"That was nice, thanks," she said as she gathered up the dirty plates to carry inside.

"It's always nice when the three of us are together," John replied.

Amberly knew it was a small dig, but she ignored it. "Yes, it is always nice," she agreed. "It's nice you and I have been able to remain on such friendly terms for Max's sake."

He was silent as he followed her into the kitchen, but it wasn't a comfortable silence. Rather, it was one that usually preceded a new plea for reconciliation between the two of them.

She hoped that wasn't the case this time. She was too tired to deal with old history, with the knowledge that she'd never been able to be what John wanted, what he needed in his life.

But it seemed whenever she and John were alone together, he couldn't help himself; he turned the conversation to the possibility of reconciliation.

"You know I miss you," he said as they put the dinner things away in the kitchen.

"John, you need to move on." She stepped over to the sliding-glass door, where she could see Max in the yard next door playing catch with his friend. She turned back to her ex-husband. "Find a nice woman, a woman who makes you happy and will be a good addition to Max's circle of family. You *have* to move on, John."

"You haven't," he returned, his dark eyes holding hers intently.

"I haven't moved forward, but I'm not going backward, either," she said gently. "John, we gave it our best shot and both of us were miserable." She reached out and placed her hand on his arm. "We were always meant to be friends, not lovers."

"I never believed that," he protested. "You were my muse, my beautiful Indian princess. The first time I painted you, I knew you were going to be somebody important in my life."

"And I am," she replied as she pulled her hand away from him. "I'm the mother of your son, and nothing and nobody can ever change that, but you have to stop thinking that somehow in the future, you and I are going to be a couple again."

"I can always hope," he replied, but thankfully his tone was lighter than it had been, and there was a spark of her old friend in his eyes. "I'd like you to come to the art show next month," he continued. "I've got a surprise that I painted for you."

"Oh God, please tell me you didn't paint me naked on a horse again."

He laughed. In the first year of their marriage, although she'd never posed for him nude, he'd painted her image looking every inch the proud Indian princess who just happened to be naked on the back of her horse.

She'd never allowed him to display it or try to sell it, and she hoped it was still in the back of the closet in the master bedroom where she'd insisted he put it after she'd seen it.

"No nude horseback riding. But I think you'll like it a lot."

"Do I have to wait until the night of the show to see it? Is it finished and can I see it now?"

He laughed again. "You never did have a lot of patience, especially when it comes to receiving gifts."

"Duh, I am a woman," she replied.

He frowned thoughtfully. "Maybe now would be a good time to give it to you. Hang tight and I'll be right back." He disappeared from the kitchen, and once again Amberly glanced out the window to check on Max.

She had several paintings from John and knew each of them was worth a small fortune. He'd already been a successful artist when she'd met him, but in the past several years he'd become something of a superstar in the Western art world.

She knew he was making tons of money from his work, but he lived a simple life and was most happy in the spare room of this modest house, which was his studio.

Turning her back to the window as she heard John's approach, she saw that he carried a medium-size canvas, the front of it against his chest.

As he turned it around for her to see, her breath caught in her throat. It was a painting of her in a red, overstuffed chair, with Max on her lap. His arms were wrapped around her, and John had captured the absolute purity of the love between mother and son.

"Oh John," she said softly. "It's absolutely amazing." His attention to detail was meticulous, and the painting seemed to breathe with life.

"Consider it an early birthday present," he said.

"My birthday is still months away," she replied as

she took the painting from him. There was a part of her that knew she shouldn't accept anything from John, that knew she shouldn't feed into his fantasy of having them back all together as a family, but she couldn't deny herself the pleasure of the picture.

"Thank you," she said. "I'll hang it in my bedroom where it's the first thing I see when I open my eyes in the morning." She turned and looked toward the window, not wanting to see the recriminations in John's eyes, the neediness that had arisen in him since their divorce and had never gone away. "I'd better get the munchkin home. I imagine he has homework and he'll need a good bath before bedtime."

She turned back around to face John. "I'll take him to school in the morning and then get in touch with you sometime during the day to see what the plans will be for tomorrow night."

He nodded. "Must be a big case. You're working lots of hours."

"It is," she replied and offered no more. "Thanks, John, for the dinner, the painting and all your support with Max," she said as she walked toward the front door.

"You know I'm here for you, Amberly. Whatever you need, whenever you need it. I've been here for you since the first day we met, and nothing has ever changed for me."

"Then I'll let you know tomorrow if I'll be available to get Max home from school." She murmured a good-bye and left, breathing a deep sigh as she walked around the side of the house to holler for Max.

It hurt her to see him so sad, to know that she was

the reason for his pain, that she was responsible for his dreams for his family not coming true.

She shoved thoughts of John out of her mind as, a few minutes later, she and Max walked into their house.

"Homework?" she asked.

"I don't have any," he replied. "Tomorrow is a first-of-the-school-year field day."

"Field day? I thought that was usually at the end of the school year, not at the beginning," she said.

"Now we have both. The first one is so us kids all get to know each other. I'm going to win all the races and get lots of ribbons."

"You know that winning isn't the most important thing. The important thing is that you do the best you can."

Max gave her a long-suffering look. "But Mom, you don't get a ribbon for doing the best you can."

Amberly laughed and pulled him into her arms. "True, but you do get a ginormous kiss from your mom." She smacked him on the forehead and then, for good measure, planted another kiss on his cheek.

"Uck, now head for the shower. Those kisses tasted like dirty boy."

Max giggled as he ran for the hall bathroom, and the sound of his giggles washed away the lingering unease that had been with her since her nightmare the night before.

As he disappeared into the bathroom, she went into her own room and stripped off the clothes she had worn for the past two days. She pulled on an old sundress, deciding she'd take a nice, long bath once Max was in bed.

She had the perfect spot on the wall opposite her bed for the painting that John had given her. It truly would be the first thing she saw when she got out of bed in the mornings.

She wished John would let go of any fantasy he entertained of them eventually finding their way back to each other. She'd told him in every way possible that it wasn't going to happen, that their marriage should have never really happened in the first place.

On impulse, she returned to the kitchen, dug her cell phone out of her purse and called her friend and fellow coworker, Lexie Forbes, who had recently become Lexie Walker. She'd met her husband almost a year ago when her sister had been murdered and she'd traveled to the small town of Widow Creek to investigate. Nick had helped her through the trauma of losing her twin sister, and in the process, the two had fallen madly in love. Nick had sold his ranch and moved to Kansas City, and two months ago, the two had married in a modest ceremony.

Lexie answered on the second ring. "I just figured I'd check on the newlyweds. How is it going?"

"I'm in a constant state of amazement and wedded bliss," Lexie replied. "What about you? What's going on?"

For the next few minutes Amberly told Lexie about her case in Mystic Lake. At one point, she walked down the hallway to check in on Max, who was in the process of drying off and getting on his pajamas.

She returned to the kitchen, where he wouldn't be able to hear her conversation with Lexie. "So, tell me more about this Sheriff Cole Caldwell," Lexie said.

"Why?"

"Because every time you mention his name, your voice lowers and gets softer. I sense something there."

Amberly laughed. "That's just your newlywed need to see romance everywhere. Granny Nightsong would say you have the blindness of happy sex in your eyes."

"I think you could use a little happy sex in your life," Lexie replied.

Amberly hated the way her thoughts instantly shot to Cole Caldwell. At that moment, Max came into the kitchen. "Hey, Lex, I've got to go. I need to spend a little time with the most important man in my life."

"Tell Max I said hi, and good luck on the case."

"Thanks, I think we're going to need all the luck we can get."

After hanging up with Lexie, Amberly and Max sat at the table and played three games of Go Fish. Amberly won one and Max won the other two, and then it was bedtime for Max.

As usual, as she sat on the edge of Max's bed and touched the charm that hung around his neck, her heart welled up with a love that nearly brought tears to her eyes.

"May the warm winds of heaven blow softly upon your house. May the Great Spirit bless all who enter here. May your moccasins make happy tracks in many snows, and may the rainbow always touch your shoulder." The old Cherokee blessing fell from her lips as she stroked several strands of his dark hair away from his forehead.

"I like that prayer," he murmured sleepily.

"I do, too." She leaned forward and kissed his forehead and then stood. "And I hope your moccasins run fast tomorrow during field day."

Max smiled, his eyes closing to what she knew would be happy dreams.

Amberly left his bedroom and headed for the master bathroom off her bedroom. She ran a tub full of hot, scented water, twisted her thick hair into a messy top-knot and then stripped off the sundress and eased into the tub.

The water enveloped her in the sweet aroma of or-chids, and the heat eased each and every muscle in her body. She tried to empty her mind, but the images of the crime-scene photos kept sliding back into her conscious-ness.

Four victims. Three potential suspects. Were they on the right track with Jeff Maynard, Jimmy Tanner and Raymond Ross? Or were they spinning their wheels chasing three lowlifes whose biggest crimes were drink-ing too much and sleeping around?

Certainly the evidence pointed that all three men hated Gretchen Johnson and might have had something to do with her death. Jimmy Tanner had slept with Bar-bara Tillman and might have had reason to get rid of her. But Mary had no real connection to any of the men.

She sank lower in the water and closed her eyes, trying to find an escape from everything, but the vic-tims refused to leave her alone. Gretchen Johnson, found next to the pizza parlor. Mary Mathis, her body on dis-play in front of the library. Barbara Tillman had appeared to rest peacefully in the city park in the shade of a big oak tree. And finally the latest, Casey Richards, shoved in between two trash bins in the back of an alleyway.

Leaning forward, she grabbed a soapy sponge and ran it across the top of her shoulders, her brain still clicking and whirling despite her tiredness.

As she washed off, the crime-scene photos flashed in her head, a slide show of horror that held her by the throat, making it nearly impossible to enjoy the luxury of her bath.

By the time she was out of the tub and clad in her nightshirt, she was certain that Casey Richards was an anomaly…a copycat murder.

She had two choices, wait until morning to let Cole know her thoughts or call him now to give him her theory. She decided it was important enough to warrant a phone call. And she told herself it had absolutely nothing to do with the fact that she wouldn't mind hearing the sound of his deep voice right now.

Back in the kitchen, she picked up her cell phone from the table and dialed his number. A glance at the clock let her know it was almost ten. She hoped he hadn't already gone to bed. They'd been putting in some killer hours the past couple of days.

He answered on the second ring. "Amberly? Is everything all right?"

She liked the sound of her unusual name falling from his lips. "Everything is fine," she quickly assured him, then added, "Well, not completely fine. Maybe I'm over-thinking things, but I don't think Casey was killed by our man."

He remained silent and she knew he was waiting for

her to continue to explain. "Think about it. The others were laid out in plain sight, posed in almost peaceful positions so they would be found immediately. He wanted his work on display, to be admired. But Casey was shoved between two trash bins in the back of an alley as if he didn't want her found too soon. Why the sudden difference?"

"A copycat." His tone was flat. "I don't know why we didn't see it immediately."

"Because we weren't looking for it. Because we'd been functioning on autopilot by the time Casey's body was found," she replied.

"I talked to her boyfriend, Terry Banks. He seemed really broken up about her death, but I need to look at him a little more closely now. I didn't initially go hard on him because I thought Casey was another random victim of our killer."

She heard the frustration in his voice, could imagine the tense lines that radiated down the sides of his handsome face, across his broad forehead.

Immediately, her desire was to erase those stress lines, even though she couldn't see them in person. "So, we investigate Casey's death as a separate murder and continue to push forward on the bigger investigation."

"Of course, you're right," he agreed. "You know what the morning headline was on our little local throw paper? Dream Catcher Killer Strikes Again, and it details Casey's murder." This time his voice was filled with disgust.

"But that could work in your favor in solving Casey's murder. Whoever killed her will feel safe."

"You're right again," he agreed, his voice a bit more relaxed than it had been moments before. "You should be in bed. We've probably got another long day ahead of us tomorrow."

"I could say the same for you," she replied and tried to force the vision of the two of them in bed together out of her head.

"Yeah, I'm heading there right now."

"Then I'll see you in the morning around nine," she replied. She hung up but remained seated at the table with her cell phone still in her hand, as if she was reluctant to break the momentary contact she'd had with him.

With a sigh, she set the cell phone on the table, feeling like a ridiculous teenager who was about to spy on her boyfriend's house in the hopes of catching just a glimpse of him.

What on earth was going on with her when it came to Cole Caldwell? She'd never before felt the ball of tension that burned inside her stomach when talking to the man. She'd never experienced a teenage crush, and that's what she felt she had going on with the handsome sheriff. But she wasn't a teenager. She was thirty years old, and her only relationship with Cole Caldwell should be as a helpmate to get a killer off the streets.

She went to bed, but it took her a long time to fall asleep as she played and replayed the kiss she'd shared with Cole, as she remembered that moment in his guest bedroom when he'd awakened her from her nightmare and sexual tension had crackled in the air between them.

It was nothing more than a crush, and crushes passed. She fell asleep with that comforting thought in mind. She awakened the next morning just after dawn, feeling well rested and ready to take on a new day.

She made coffee, sucked down her first cup of the day and then decided to make pancakes for breakfast for her and Max. She got out the griddle, made the batter and then drank a second cup of coffee as she watched the sunrise.

As she stood at the window, she once again found her thoughts going back to the murders. Cole had instructed one of his deputies to run a search to see if dream catchers had been noted at any other murders in the general area over the past year. They'd also researched everything they could find about dream catchers in Indian culture, but had come up with no reason that the dream catchers might have been left at the murder scenes.

Whatever meaning the dream catchers had to the killer remained a mystery, but somehow, Amberly felt if they could solve that puzzle, it would go a long way in finding the killer. She wasn't sure she believed that the killer hung them in order to keep the dead from having nightmares. There had to be another reason.

At quarter to seven, she went into Max's bedroom to wake him. He was one of those kids who awoke instantly and always with a smile on his face. There was never any prodding or poking to get him up; he bounded out of bed as if in anticipation of a great adventure.

"Pancakes will be ready by the time you're dressed," she said.

"Chocolate chip?" he asked eagerly.

She smiled. "I think we can arrange a sprinkling of chips on each pancake," she agreed.

"Awesome," Max exclaimed as he headed to the hall bathroom.

By seven-fifteen, they were seated at the table sharing breakfast, and Max told her everything that was going to happen at school that day and his hopes to bring home at least half a dozen ribbons for activities during field day.

"If you wind up going to your dad's after school today, I'll call and you can give me the final medal total."

"Expect to be amazed," Max said, a shiny string of syrup running down his mouth.

Amberly laughed and handed him a napkin. "Finish up, brush your teeth and then grab your backpack. We've got to hit the road in ten minutes."

As Max disappeared into the bathroom once again, Amberly quickly cleared the breakfast mess and then gathered her keys and purse to wait by the door. Within minutes, Max had joined her, and together they walked out into the morning sunshine.

"Hey, Ed," she greeted her neighbor, who was in the process of digging up a dead shrub at the corner of his house. "You're up and at it early this morning."

"Heard it was supposed to get hot later today, and I've been meaning to get this eyesore out of here for the last year. Figured there was no better time than this minute. I want it gone before winter sets in." He leaned on the handle of the shovel and smiled at Max. "Gonna knock them all dead today at field day, sport?"

"Definitely. I've got on my fastest tennis shoes and my lucky necklace." He grabbed the amulet that hung around his neck. "Nobody stands a chance against me!"

"You'll be at your dad's after school today?" Ed asked.

Max exchanged a glance with his mother. "Probably. Mom's working a big case."

"Then I'll probably see you over there. I'm determined to beat your dad at at least two games of chess in a row," Ed said.

"Okay, see ya later," Max said as he ran to the car.

"You are John are playing chess a lot in the evenings," Amberly said to Ed.

"He's a lonely man, Amberly."

"I know. I've told him to move on, to find some nice woman who he can build something with," Amberly said in frustration.

Ed nodded. "I've told him the same thing, only I told him to make her a blonde this time."

Amberly laughed. "I've got to get out of here. See you later, Ed."

As he waved a hand and then went back to digging with the shovel, she hurried toward her car in the driveway. She had just pulled out of her driveway when she noticed it, and her blood ran icy cold in her veins.

The dream catcher hung from her mailbox, and attached below it was a photo of her. She hit the brakes and put the car in Park, afraid to move, fear screaming through her so loud it took her several minutes to hear Max in the seat next to her.

"Mom, what's wrong? Aren't we going to school?"

He knew where she lived. He or they had left this as a warning that she was vulnerable, and that made Max vulnerable. Max... She had to get Max out of here. She dug her cell phone out of her purse and called John.

She didn't want to leave her position in front of the

mailbox, was somehow afraid that if she left for even a moment, then while she was gone, this new evidence would magically disappear.

John agreed to meet her at her house and get Max to school. The next call she made was to Cole. He answered on the first ring. "I have a problem," she said.

"What kind of problem?"

"I was just getting ready to drive Max to school and I saw a dream catcher and my photo hanging on my mailbox," she said.

There was a long moment of stunned silence. "Don't touch anything and don't call the local cops. I'll be there in twenty minutes. This is part of our ongoing investigation. I don't want anyone else involved."

Before she could say anything else, he clicked off. By that time, John had arrived. It took only a minute to transfer Max from her car to his, and then he roared off, promising to be back after he'd dropped Max at school.

Ed watched the proceedings but kept his own counsel, continuing to dig at the shrub while Amberly focused her attention back on the dream catcher and photo.

The picture was a profile photo from one of the social networks she occasionally visited, and the dream catcher, the cheap kind that had been found at all of the crime scenes in Mystic Lake.

Was this the work of one of the men she'd met in the bar Friday night? The same night she'd thought somebody had been outside of her house?

Was this a reminder to her that they could get to her whenever they wanted, or was this a promise that she was intended to be the next victim?

## Chapter Seven

Cole pressed his foot on the gas pedal, the strobes on the top of his car shooting out brilliant cherry lights in all directions as the piercing siren blared for everyone on the road to get out of his way.

The killer knew where Amberly lived. The words reverberated around and around in his head as his stomach muscles twisted with raw anxiety. He knew where she lived and he'd left her a calling card.

How had this happened? How had he allowed this to happen? He felt the same impotent rage that he'd felt when Emily had been kidnapped and he'd known he'd been the one who had invited danger into her life.

She'd always told him that she knew what she'd signed up for when she'd married a cop, but that hadn't eased his sense of guilt when she'd been killed.

Was it possible that the same copycat who had killed Casey Richards was just having fun with Amberly? Playing some kind of a sick game?

Prank, or very real, dangerous threat? He couldn't take the risk of finding out what the truth was; if he guessed wrong it was Amberly's very life that hung in the balance.

He hadn't expected this. None of the other victims had been forewarned. If it was the killer, then he was acting out of character and that scared Cole half to death. There was no way to second-guess a killer who changed the rules in the middle of a game.

Traffic fell to the sides of the highway, allowing him to zoom ahead unimpeded. There were definitely benefits to driving a patrol car blazing and screaming through the streets.

Amberly had thought somebody had been outside of her house Friday night after she'd left Mystic Lake. She'd thought it might have been one of the three men from Bledsoe's. Was one of them the killer? Had he followed her home? Had she led him right to the very place that should be her safe haven?

The GPS system in his vehicle gave him the directions straight to her address, and he couldn't get there fast enough. He felt a little bit like he had when he'd rushed to the scene where Emily had been being held by Jeb Wilson, a man who had killed his family and whom Cole had been hunting.

Timing was everything. What if the killer was still there on the scene? Hiding out? Just waiting for the perfect opportunity to strike?

One thing was clear. Amberly and her son were no longer safe in their own home. He exited off the highway and onto a main thoroughfare that would lead him to her neighborhood.

He didn't want the Kansas City law enforcement involved in this, although he knew that he might be stepping on toes. This was his investigation, and in truth, leaving a dream catcher and a picture on a mailbox wasn't a crime—unless it was tied into what was happening in his small town.

He didn't want the mess of interacting with another police department. It wasn't that he was selfish or arrogant—he just knew the kind of hoops and red tape that would come with involving anyone else. He'd been there, done that, and with dreadful results.

A left turn off the main road led him into a nice neighborhood with well-kept homes and lawns. He spied Amberly's car parked in front of an attractive brick ranch house.

She was out of her car, talking to a man who apparently was the next-door neighbor. Cole pulled up behind her car and got out, grateful to see that she was okay.

"That didn't take long," she said as he approached where she and the other man stood in the center of the front yard.

"It's amazing how fast you can move with a siren and a light on your car." He looked at her neighbor. "Sheriff Cole Caldwell," he said as he held out his hand.

"Ed Gershner." He gave Cole's hand a firm shake. The man had short, dark hair with gray sprinkled here and there. He looked like a man who spent a lot of time outdoors, his long face and arms bronzed by the sun. The only distinctive thing Cole noticed was a large mole on his collarbone that his half-unbuttoned short-sleeved shirt displayed.

"I was just telling Amberly here that I didn't see or hear anything unusual last night, but I'm an early-to-bed kind of man, and I sleep pretty hard."

"Ed came out this morning just after seven to start some yard work. He didn't pay any attention to my mailbox, so we can assume the things were placed there sometime during the night," Amberly said.

Cole walked over to the mailbox to have a closer look. His gut burned with an icy fire as he saw the photo of Amberly connected to the dream catcher with a piece of ordinary string.

He looked back at her. "Have you checked the house thoroughly to make sure none of the windows or doors or anything else have been tampered with?"

He hated the way her eyes darkened and sparked with a new fear. She obviously hadn't thought of any other safety issues or potential invasions into her privacy.

"Come on, let's take a walk around the house and check things out," he said to Amberly. "Nice to meet you, Ed. I may have some more questions for you later."

"I'll be here," Ed replied as he ambled toward his garage.

Amberly turned dark eyes to Cole as they headed for the side of the house. "I never thought about anyone trying to jimmy windows or doors," she said worriedly. "I didn't hear anything in the night, but I slept hard."

"And whoever left that on the mailbox probably didn't get any closer to the house," he said in an attempt to reassure her. "But I'd rather be safe than sorry."

"That definitely makes two of us," she agreed.

They walked the entire perimeter of the house, checking for any signs of tampering, but found nothing. When they reached the front yard again, a car pulled up in the driveway, and a tall, handsome man got out of the driver's seat.

"Amberly," he called. "Want to let me know what's going on?"

Amberly quickly introduced the man to Cole as John Merriweather, her ex-husband. "Amberly has been working with me on a series of murders in Mystic Lake, and it appears some of that work has followed her home," Cole said. He turned to look at Amberly. "And I don't believe it's safe for her to remain in this house." He quickly explained about the dream catchers and the murders taking place twenty miles away.

"Max can stay with me," John said as he looked at Amberly. "You do what you need to do in order to clear up this mess, but until then I don't want you anywhere near him." His voice held a rough, angry edge but his eyes were conflicted. He still cared for her.

"You're absolutely right," she agreed. "He needs to stay with you, and away from me." Cole could hear the very heartbreak in her voice at the tough decision that had to be made.

Cole touched her elbow. "Why don't I go inside with you and you can gather up some clothes and whatever you need and we'll figure things out when we get to Mystic Lake?"

John Merriweather might have been an accomplished artist, but at the moment he was only a frightened, angry father, and his anger seemed to be directed at both Cole and Amberly.

"This is what always worried me," he said in a taut voice. "That, somehow, the lines between your professional life and your personal life would get blurred and put Max at risk. And now that's happened."

"John, there was no way I could foresee something like this," she protested.

"And there's no reason to believe that your son is in any danger. This man targets young women, not children," Cole said firmly.

"Just call me when you have this mess cleaned up." John didn't wait for her response, but got back into his car and squealed out of the driveway.

"Whew, he's kind of intense, isn't he?" Cole said in an effort to break the tension.

"Not usually, but he's angry. He's always hated my job. This only makes everything he believed about it seem right."

"I meant what I said about Max. I don't believe he's in any danger. There's nothing to indicate that our killer has suddenly decided to target children. This was intended for you and nobody else."

She nodded and cast him a grateful smile. "Thank you. I needed to hear that."

"Let me collect the evidence, and then we'll get your things." She watched as he returned to his car and pulled out a pair of gloves, a camera and an evidence envelope.

She took the camera from him, and while she snapped photos of the mailbox decorations, he pulled on the pair of gloves. Within minutes, the dream catcher and photo were in the envelope, and he and Amberly entered her house.

His first impression was one of inviting warmth. Rich hardwood floors were covered by a thick Native American rug patterned in bright colors. Interesting-looking pottery sat on the fireplace mantel, and the sofa was an earth-brown and decorated with yellow, red and orange throw pillows, which matched the rug.

The décor reflected her, not just her heritage but her warmth. There was a sense of love here, a sense of family, even though he knew it was just her and her son.

He followed her through the living room and down the hallway. They passed what he assumed was Max's room, painted a dark blue and with a variety of law-enforcement posters and emblems on the walls.

He could smell her bedroom before they reached it, that exotic scent that had teased his senses since the moment he'd met her.

Her room was not frilly, and he hadn't expected it to be. She wasn't a frilly kind of woman. The bedspread was deep green, and the curtains at the window were beige with a thin green stripe. The top of the dresser held an array of photographs of Max at various ages, but it was the painting hanging on the wall opposite the bed that drew him.

It was obviously a John Merriweather, and it was equally obvious that love had been in each brush stroke. The subject of the painting was Amberly and Max, and John had done an amazing job capturing two of the people who were obviously very important in his life.

Amberly grabbed a large suitcase from the closet and began to fill it with clothes. He leaned against the door-jamb and watched, unsure what to say to alleviate the fear, the pain that must be roaring through her at the moment.

She was not only having to abandon her home but also leave her son, because somebody was playing games... potentially deadly games.

"You lied to me when you told me your bedroom was nothing more than a bed and a dresser," he said to break the silence. "I pictured a bare mattress on the floor."

She flashed him a tense smile. "I still want to paint the walls in here, a nice pale green, and I've had that bedspread for the last ten years. This just feels like my uncompleted room in the house."

It didn't take her long to fill the suitcase, then pull out an overnight bag and disappear into her bathroom. He didn't want to think about how frightened he'd been to see that dream catcher hanging over her picture, but he knew one thing clearly—he didn't want to let her out of his sight...not now...not until they had the killer behind bars.

"I'd like you to drive back to Mystic Lake in my car and have you stay in my guest room until we get to the bottom of all this," he said.

She stuck her head out of the bathroom door, her expression one of surprise. "I just assumed I'd park myself at a motel someplace in the area."

"I don't want you alone anywhere," he replied. "I'd feel more comfortable with the buddy system, and I want my buddy under my roof."

She disappeared back into the bathroom without answering. Was she remembering that moment in his guest room when he'd awakened her from her nightmare?

His desire to keep her close had nothing to do with

any lust he might feel for her; it had everything to do with his need to keep her safe and sound.

She exited the bathroom with her overnight bag. "Okay, I'm in for staying at your place." Her gaze didn't quite meet his, and he thought he saw a tremble possess her lower lip.

"This shook you up pretty badly," he said softly.

Her gaze met his. "I'd be lying if I said anything else." She sank down on the edge of the bed and set her bag next to her. "Seeing it right here, in the place where I live, in the place where my son sleeps and eats... I don't think I've really processed it until now, while I'm packing up to leave everything."

He heard the emotion in her voice, thick and raw, and he wasn't sure if it was fear or sadness or a combination of both. "It's going to be all right," he said as he shifted from one foot to the other. "We're going to get this guy."

She nodded, her head still down. She looked broken, and he ached for her. From the moment he'd met her, he'd noticed she radiated an inner strength, a wealth of spirit that drew him to her. But he found himself equally drawn to the woman seated on the bed, who looked like she needed nothing more than a pair of strong arms around her.

He walked over to stand directly in front of her. "Amberly," he said softly.

She looked up at him then, and her beautiful brown eyes were filled with tears. He opened his arms, and she shot off the bed and into them as if she'd just been waiting for him to make the offer.

She didn't cry although she relaxed completely against

him and rested her head in the crook of his shoulder as if finding his arms the most peaceful place on the face of the earth.

He tried not to notice the fragrance that wafted from her hair, the fullness of her breasts pressed against his chest and her heart beating against his own.

The last thing he wanted was for his body to react inappropriately to the moment, but he seemed to lose control when she was around.

She was all soft curves and sweet-scented femininity, and just before he feared he might embarrass himself, he dropped his arms from around her and stepped back. "Okay?" he asked.

Although her eyes remained dark, she straightened her shoulders and lifted her chin. "I'm fine, and the sooner we catch this bastard the better." She picked up her purse and her overnight bag while Cole grabbed her suitcase, and together they left the house.

Ed was still outside, pruning some of the bushes in front of his walkway. "Ed, I'm going to be gone for a little while. Would you keep an eye on the house for me?" Amberly asked.

"Of course I will, and I'll help John with the little guy, too," he replied.

"I appreciate it," she replied, emotion once again thick in her voice.

Minutes later, they were in Cole's car and headed to his home in Mystic Lake. "Maybe we got lucky, and we'll find some fingerprints on the dream catcher or on the photo of you," he said, breaking the silence that had become too long between them.

"You don't believe that," she replied flatly. "He's not about to make that kind of mistake. He hasn't left prints at any of the other scenes. Unless he's some kind of copycat, he won't have screwed up this one by getting careless."

"Sooner or later, he's got to make a mistake," Cole replied, a burn in the pit of his stomach.

"Let's hope it's sooner rather than later. I can't put my life with Max on hold forever." Her fingers laced tightly together in her lap.

"You were right. He's a cute kid." He felt her curious gaze on him. "I saw the pictures of him on top of your dresser and the painting that John did of the two of you."

"He'll be just fine with John," she replied, obviously more to convince herself than him.

"I gather John doesn't like what you do for a living."

She released a dry laugh. "You think?" She relaxed against the seat and released a deep sigh. "John and I were never meant to be married."

"How did the two of you meet?" There was no question he was intrigued about her past. It made her the woman she was today.

"We met in a coffee shop. He approached me to ask if he could paint me. I thought he was some kind of a creep and blew him off, but he gave me a card, and later that day I looked him up on the internet and realized he was the real deal. I was intrigued, so I agreed to be his model, and we struck up a wonderful friendship."

"And that friendship turned into love?"

"Not exactly, although I wish it would have been that easy."

He shot her a quick glance and noted the frown that danced across her features. "One night, John sold a large painting for more money than he'd ever sold one for before. We celebrated with a bottle of champagne and before the night was over, Max was conceived. When John found out I was pregnant, he insisted we get married. Coming from a broken family, I didn't want a baby out of wedlock. I wanted Max to have a whole family, together, so I said yes. I thought we could make it work, but it was the worst mistake I've ever made."

He glanced at her again and then focused back on the road. "Mistake, how?"

She paused for a long moment and looked out the passenger window. "We weren't meant to be married. I felt no passion for John. Any passion I've ever felt in my life was for my job and, of course, now Max. But not for John, not for anybody else."

"Did he feel passion toward you?" Cole couldn't imagine a man with a beating heart who wouldn't.

"Sometimes, I think too much. John was in love with me. I loved John, but I wasn't in love with him."

"I'm guessing he didn't want the divorce?"

"What John wanted more than anything in the world was for us to stay married and me to become the woman he needed in his life. He wanted me to quit my job, be mommy and wife during the day and his artistic muse and lover in the evenings. He needed me to be something I'm not, and the longer we stayed together, the more miserable we both became, and so I decided to pull the plug. He's been trying to get me to reconsider ever since." She released a deep sigh. "I just want him to be happy."

"And you wouldn't reconsider and go back to him?" He pulled into his driveway and cut the engine.

"Never," she said firmly. "I don't really believe in passion that never cools, that marriage doesn't somehow suck the life out of one of the partners. Somebody has to give too much, become less than what they are, for it to really work."

He pulled his keys from the ignition and turned to look at her. "Hopefully, someday in your life, you'll find the man to prove you wrong. Now, let's get you unpacked, and then we have a killer to catch."

As he got out of the car he glanced around the area, his gun at his hip, ready to be drawn if he saw anything unusual. What worried him most about the items left on Amberly's mailbox was the fact that he didn't know if they'd been left there as a prank, a threat or a deadly promise.

## Chapter Eight

Amberly felt as if the rest of the day went by in a gray fog. It didn't take her long to unpack her things in Cole's guest bedroom and take over the hall bathroom with her toiletries, and as she did, she remained curiously numb.

It was only when she set a small framed picture of Max on the nightstand next to the bed that the grief and rage pierced the fog.

How dare he come to her home, displace her and make her worry about the safety of her child? How dare he force a situation where she had to distance herself from the one person she loved more than any other on the face of the earth?

She was seated on the edge of the bed when Cole knocked on the door and peeked in. "You want to just hang out here for the rest of the day, kind of get your feet beneath you?"

"Absolutely not." She stood. "I want to spend every minute of every hour that I possibly can trying to catch this creep."

"I thought that's what you'd say," he said, a hint of approval warming his blue eyes. "I've set up an interview at the office in about twenty minutes with Terry Banks,

Casey's boyfriend at the time of her murder. I'm assuming you'd like to be there."

"Absolutely," she agreed and followed him out of the room. They were quiet on the ride to the office. The only emotion that radiated in the car was the frustration coming off both of them.

"Do you think it's possible that the three men are working together to commit these murders?" she asked.

He knew immediately what three men she was asking about. "It would definitely be unusual in the world of serial killers to have three involved. But there's no question that Raymond, Jimmy and Jeff are tight. They're alibiing each other for two of the murders…both Gretchen's and Barbara's."

She looked at him in surprise and he continued. "After you left to go home last night I gathered the three of them into separate rooms to find out about their alibis on the nights of the other murders. They each had separate alibis for Mary's murder but once again insisted that on the nights that Gretchen and Barbara were killed, they were all at Raymond's house playing poker."

"They play poker a lot," she said dryly. "I wonder what other games they like to play."

"The last thing we should do is indulge in that tunnel-vision thinking you mentioned before. Those three men are definitely at the top of our suspect list, but without any real concrete evidence to prove their involvement, we need to keep searching and keep our options open."

"I agree. I just wish somebody else would pop up on our radar." She was determined to stay focused on the case and not allow herself to think about what it had just taken away from her—time with Max.

By the time they got to his office, Lana Scott, the daytime receptionist, informed them that Terry Banks had arrived and was in the small interrogation room with Deputy Black.

Amberly followed Cole into the room and found Roger Black standing against the wall and Terry Banks seated at the small table, an open can of soda in front of him. He jumped up at the sight of them, his hazel eyes glassy and slightly wild.

"Sheriff, I don't understand. Why am I here?" he asked, his voice cracking with either nerves or some other emotion.

"Sit down, Terry, I just have a few more questions for you."

Terry sank back down on the chair. Amberly knew he was twenty-one years old, but he looked achinglsy young. His brown hair looked as if it hadn't seen a comb in days, and he sported a patch of acne on his chin.

Casey had been the youngest victim. She'd been twenty years old, another anomaly in the pattern the killer had established so far.

As Cole gave Terry his Miranda rights, Terry insisted he didn't need a lawyer or anyone else. Suspects could be arrogantly stupid when it came to their rights, Amberly thought. If she faced an interrogation by a man like Cole, she'd definitely want a lawyer standing by her side.

She stood against the wall next to Roger as Cole began to question the young man. Cole took the chair across from Terry, and for a few minutes, the conversation was easy as Terry talked about his grief over Casey's death.

They'd been dating since high school and had plans to get married as soon as they got financially on their feet. Amberly watched with interest as Cole played the role of friend and father confessor and slowly morphed into a stern figure of authority.

He played the kid like a fiddle, with force and finesse, and within thirty minutes, Terry was sobbing like a baby and confessing that he'd killed Casey, but it had all been an accident, a horrible accident.

"We got into a fight and I pushed her. She fell and hit her head on the coffee table. I didn't see any blood, but when I tried to wake her, when I felt for her pulse, I realized she wasn't breathing, that she was dead." The words sobbed out of him, his eyes pleading with each and every one of them to understand.

"I freaked, and all I could think about were the murders that already happened, so I figured I'd stage the scene to make it look like Casey had been murdered by the same guy." He wiped snot and slobber off his face with the back of his arm. "I...I had to stab her to make it look right and then I went to the Dollar Store and bought one of those dream things and then I took her to the alley." He lowered his head into his hands and continued to cry.

Amberly tried to work up a little bit of sympathy for him, but it wasn't there. He should have dialed 911 the moment she'd hit the floor and had been unconscious. Terry Banks wasn't a doctor—he had no way of knowing if paramedics might have been able to save Casey.

He was just a stupid kid who had taken a bad situation and made it far worse.

Cole placed the kid under arrest, and Deputy Black led him out of the room. Amberly smiled at Cole as the two of them were left alone in the room.

"You handled him like an expert interrogator. You know just when to push and just when to pull back." She knew her admiration was in her tone of voice and he deserved it.

She was surprised when his cheeks took on a dusky shade of embarrassment. "The kid was ready to confess to whoever asked him the right questions. I didn't do anything so special."

She would have argued with him, but he moved toward the door. "I need to check with the coroner and get the full autopsy on Casey. We need to make sure that this was truly a badly covered-up accident and not cold-blooded murder. At this point, I'm not into believing anything anyone tells me."

The rest of the day dragged by. Amberly spent much of the day in the war room, reading and rereading reports and staring at the crime-scene photos as she tried to get into the head of the killer. While she holed up in the room, Cole worked the streets, contacting people for second and third interviews.

There was no question that the key to the killer was in the dream catchers. Being a Native American herself and having a dream catcher above Max's head when he slept at night made this particular puzzle feel oddly personal.

She wished her granny Nightsong was still alive. She'd

always taken her problems and worries to Granny, who had managed to give her clarity and had always found the humor in any situation.

But she had a feeling even Granny Nightsong wouldn't have had any wisdom to give when it came to these murders. And she definitely wouldn't have been able to find any humor in the deaths of such vibrant, young women.

It was nearly seven in the evening when Cole finally returned to the room. He sank down in the chair opposite hers. "You doing okay?"

She nodded and pulled a strand of her hair over her shoulder and toyed with the ends. "I'm fine. I was just sitting here wondering what my granny Nightsong would say about all this."

He leaned back in his chair, the tired lines in his face relaxing slightly. "And what would she have said?"

Amberly frowned thoughtfully. "She would have said that the Raven Mocker is after me."

"The Raven Mocker?"

"He's the most dreaded of all the Cherokee witches. In legend, he flies into the house of somebody who is dying and steals their life. He eats their heart, and that adds to his life however old the person was that he took. But Granny Nightsong believed the Raven Mocker was more than just an evil entity that preyed on the sick and dying. She believed Raven Mockers were responsible for all murders and untimely deaths that occurred."

"So, there's more than one Raven Mocker?"

"There are many, and only a Cherokee medicine man has the power to drive them away."

"Maybe we should hire one to help us with this case," he said dryly.

"Maybe we should just order a pizza instead."

He laughed, and she realized it was the first time she'd heard a real, honest burst of laughter from him. The warmth of the sound wrapped around her, stealing in to heat the cold that had invaded her since the moment she'd seen the things on her mailbox.

"Now, that sounds like a plan," he agreed. "We've been working this pretty intensely since the moment you signed on. We need a little break to get some distance from everything and hope that distance gives us a new perspective. Pizza and beer sound like the perfect answer."

Within minutes, they were in his car and headed for his house. For the first time in days, they spoke of inconsequential things—the warm weather which was lingering, the growth of the Kansas City area and the popularity of reality shows on television.

It was the first time they'd talked about anything but the crimes and what little they'd shared of their personal lives. It was pleasant just to enjoy a conversation that kept her mind away from murder and Max.

They arrived at Cole's house, and by the time she'd changed into a comfortable pair of jeans and an aqua-blue tank top, he'd ordered a large supreme pizza and set two icy bottles of beer out on the table.

He'd changed clothes, too. He sported a worn pair of jeans, which hugged his lean legs, and a white T-shirt pulled taut over his broad shoulders.

He picked up the two bottles of beer and then motioned her into the living room. "There is one rule for the rest of the night," he said as he settled down next to her on the sofa.

"Ah, you didn't mention that the accommodations here came with rules," she said teasingly.

"Only one and only for the remainder of tonight. The rule is that, for the rest of the evening, we don't talk about dream catchers or murders," he said as he twisted off the top of his bottle.

"I'll toast to that," she replied, and they clinked their bottles together. She leaned back and took a sip of the beer and watched as he did the same.

"I know I've asked this before, but remind me. Why are you working in this small town? Why not a bigger city where your skills would be better utilized?" she asked.

He leaned back against the sofa, his eyes darkening slightly. "When Emily was killed, all I wanted to do was escape. I knew I couldn't continue to live in the same house where we'd been so happy, and I knew I couldn't go back to the job that I'd been working when she'd been killed. I quit my job and lived in a motel for about three months, drinking and wallowing in grief and self-pity."

He paused to take another drink of his beer and then continued, "But you know, there's only so long you can wallow before you get sick of yourself. I couldn't face going back to working on the same police force that I'd been on, but being a cop was in my blood, so I saw a small ad for a sheriff here and I applied."

"How long were you and Emily married?"

"Three wonderful years," he replied.

"Tell me about her." Amberly wanted to know all about the woman he had married, the woman he'd loved so desperately, so passionately that he'd decided if he couldn't have her, he'd rather live the rest of his life alone.

"She was a pretty blonde, kind of quiet but with a great sense of humor. She loved two things in life, being a teacher and me, and just for your information, in the three years we were married our passion for each other never waned."

A wistful yearning filled Amberly at his words. "And how long since her death?"

"Almost eight years."

"That's a long time to be alone."

"Yes, it is." Once again he tipped his bottle to his lips, but his gaze remained locked with hers and held a spark of something hot and dangerous that caused the breath to catch in Amberly's chest.

He was looking at her the same way he had that night in his guest bedroom when she'd wanted nothing more than to invite him into her bed.

The crackling electricity was back in the air, raising the hair on the nape of her neck, forcing her heartbeat to thud a little faster.

There was want in his eyes, hot, fiery need that seemed to melt every bone in her body. He didn't move an inch closer to her, and yet she felt him invading her space, not in an intimidating way but rather like an intoxicating haze she wanted to get lost in.

At that moment the doorbell rang, and the moment shattered as the pizza arrived.

COLE RUBBED THE BACK OF his neck where tension had snarled his muscles into a tight knot. He knew that part of the tension came from the fact that in the past week they'd made no more headway on the murders. But he also knew that part of the tension was from being under the same roof as Amberly for the past seven days.

They'd fallen into a comfortable routine, sharing coffee just after dawn, heading into the office by seven and working both together and apart throughout the day.

They worked together as if they had been doing so for years, finishing each other's thoughts and anticipating each other's needs. They cooked together if there was time or ate takeout if they'd worked particularly late. They shared laughter and ancient stories about each other, but beneath it all, Cole felt a continuous simmer of desire for her.

And in the past week he'd been thinking a lot about Emily. He'd not only thought about all that he'd lost when she'd died, but also all that he'd given up as a result of her death.

Emily wouldn't have wanted him to close himself off from feeling, from loving. In fact, she would have been angry with him for cutting himself off from love, from building something special for himself with another woman.

There were so many things about being a couple he'd forgotten about, such as the noise of somebody else in his quiet space. Amberly filled the house with her sound. Wherever he was, he found himself listening for her soft footsteps, straining to hear the way she hummed slightly off-key when she stood in front of the oven.

He liked the conversations they had, whether they were talking about nothing or talking about something important. Over the past week, she'd charmed him with stories about growing up with her granny Nightsong and her son, whom he knew she missed desperately. The brief visits and phone calls she had with Max weren't enough to fill her mother soul.

He'd sent her home with Deputy Black an hour earlier, needing some distance from her. She was getting to him with her beauty and intelligence, with her lilting laughter and smoky, dark eyes.

Her scent infused the house, and each night he dreamed of her in his bed. Murder and Amberly, that's all that filled his head these days. He didn't know how to solve the murders, and he wasn't sure what to do about his desire for Amberly. Those two things caused the tension to pinch his neck and ride down his back.

A glance at his watch showed him it was just after eight. It was time to end another unproductive day. He was just about to get up from his desk when Linda buzzed to tell him Tara Tanner was there to see him. Cole told Linda to send the woman in, wondering what on earth Jimmy Tanner's wife might want to tell him.

She came into the office with blue eyes blazing and short, crackling-dry, white-blond hair nearly standing on end. "I have a bone to pick with you, Sheriff Caldwell," she exclaimed. Her body nearly vibrated with anger. "You've been harassing my husband."

"It's called investigating a murder, not harassment," Cole countered and gestured her into the chair opposite him. She refused to sit and instead began to pace in front of his desk. "Besides, I thought the two of you were divorcing."

"Malicious gossip. I have no intention of leaving Jimmy, and he's not going anywhere, either. We've been together since we were kids, and we'll die together as an old married couple. Oh, I know Jimmy is an ass who drinks too much and cheats on me, but he's my ass, and he always comes home to me. We know each other... we understand each other, and I'm telling you right now there's no way Jimmy could have anything to do with murdering those women."

She paused, and he didn't know if it was because she expected a reply from him or simply needed to catch her breath. "Tara, I'm just doing my job. Jimmy runs with a rough crowd. Both your husband and Jeff and Raymond have ties to at least two of the three victims. I can't just ignore that during my investigation."

"The Three Stooges, that's what those men are whenever they're together. Between the three of them, you couldn't find a fully functional brain." She leaned forward, bracing herself with her hands on the edge of his desk. "Every minute you're spending on Jimmy and Jeff and Raymond, you're wasting valuable time in finding the real killer."

"I'll take your concerns under advisement," he said, knowing his words wouldn't satisfy her but might move her out of his office.

She frowned in obvious disgust and, just as he'd hoped, straightened and left the room. The scent of her thick, cheap perfume still lingered when Deputy Ben Jamison walked in.

"Saw Tara Tanner storming out of here on her stiletto shoes and figured I'd better get back here to make sure she didn't stab you in the eye with the heel of one of them." He sank down on the chair opposite Cole.

Cole grinned at the deputy, who was not only his right-hand man but also had become a good friend. "No, she basically came in to tell me her husband is too stupid to be a murderer."

Ben grinned. "Can't say I disagree with her. But I don't feel the same way about Jeff. He's smart like a fox and a hothead to boot. I can imagine him offing Gretchen and then liking the kill so much he just keeps on going."

"Yeah, well, somebody is liking the kill way too much, and we need to find him before he decides to act again." Cole's gut clenched as he thought of the dream catcher and photo hanging from Amberly's mailbox.

Threat or promise? This thought kept him awake nights. Was she already marked as the next intended victim?

It was this fear that had prompted him to have Roger drive her home when she'd decided to leave earlier. And it was that same fear that would keep Roger there with her until Cole arrived home.

"We definitely could use a break," Ben said. "So far, this guy hasn't made a single mistake."

"And I'm having nightmares about every woman in town having a dream catcher hung over her head."

"Speaking of dream catchers, where's Amberly? I didn't see her when I came through the building."

"I sent her home about an hour ago. I've got Roger sitting on her until I get there. She looked tired."

"We've all been putting in a lot of extra hours in an effort to find this killer." Ben raked a hand through his thick blond hair. "It's got to be especially hard on Amberly. She must be going crazy this long without seeing her kid. Talking to him on the phone just isn't the same as being able to be with him."

"It's killing her," Cole agreed and then winced at his choice of words. "She's using a disposable cell phone to call John's house in case somehow her call can be traced. Although it's illogical, she feels like any little bit of contact might put Max in the killer's sights."

"You mentioned to me that her husband was a famous artist who didn't like her working as an FBI agent."

Cole nodded. "She told me that John wanted her to quit her job when she got married and had Max."

Ben laughed. "If she's anything like all of us, once the law-enforcement bug strikes, it never goes away. You're forever sick with the need to work in that field."

"Apparently her husband didn't understand that concept."

"Is that why they divorced?" Ben asked curiously.

"One of the reasons," Cole replied. "Although, according to Amberly, John would take her back in a minute." Cole didn't mention that Amberly had told him she'd never been in love with John, that she'd never felt that kind of passion for any man.

Still, there had been moments over the past seven days when he'd thought he'd felt that emotion simmering in her for him. There had been times when he'd desperately wanted to kiss her, when he'd sensed the same desire coming from her. But he hadn't acted on it.

What was the point? She'd made it clear that she had no intention of looking for any relationship, that she didn't want to drag men into Max's life. And while his mind was changing about what his future held, and his heart was opening to the possibility of loving again, ultimately Amberly was just a coworker, here today and gone tomorrow.

"Have you considered her ex-husband as a potential suspect?" Ben's question pulled Cole from his current thoughts. He stared at his deputy in surprise.

"Why on earth would John Merriweather be killing women in Mystic Lake?"

"I don't know, sometimes I just think crazy," Ben said with a small, dry laugh.

"Please, share your crazy thoughts with me," Cole replied, desperate to hear any theory of these crimes, no matter how outlandish.

Ben leaned back in his chair and stretched his long legs out in front of him. "I was just thinking, this guy doesn't want his ex-wife to be an FBI agent, so he kills a bunch of women here and hangs the dream catcher hoping that the FBI office in Kansas City will send Amberly because of the Native American overtones. So, she's sent to a small town where she isn't sure of her welcome, deals with heinous crimes that probably give her nightmares. Then the kicker is he hangs a picture and a dream catcher on her mailbox to make sure she's separated from her son, hoping that the experience will drive her to quit her job and ultimately drive her back into his awaiting arms."

"That would take one sick, evil mind to orchestrate all of that."

Ben grinned. "Yeah, that's why I thought of it."

Half an hour later, as Cole drove toward his house, he thought about Ben's theory. It sounded crazy, laden with the potential for failure, and yet it also held enough possibility that Cole couldn't automatically dismiss it.

Now all he had to figure out was how to tell Amberly that they had a new suspect on their list, and that suspect was her ex-husband.

How was he supposed to tell her that their newest suspect was the father of her child?

## Chapter Nine

"I just thought it was time for another check-in," Amberly said into her cell phone to Lexie.

"It's about time. How are you holding up? How's the case coming along?"

It took Amberly several minutes to catch up Lexie on everything that had happened over the past week. She sank down at the table in the kitchen, which smelled of baked chicken and homemade macaroni and cheese.

"So, you've been staying at Cole Caldwell's house? How's that working out?"

"Okay, except I miss Max desperately."

"Of course you do," Lexie said sympathetically. "But you know he's fine with John, and you've been away from him for cases before."

"I know. This just feels different because it's not something I chose, it was the manipulation of some creep." She sighed and continued, "Has Nick found work?" She knew that Nick had sold his farm in Widow Creek, the town where he'd lived when he and Lexie had met, to move with her to Kansas City so Lexie could continue her job as an FBI computer geek.

"He's considering some options," Lexie replied. "With

the sale of the farm, he really doesn't have to hurry to just find anything. I want him to find something he's passionate about, something he loves doing."

The two chatted for a few more minutes and then hung up. Amberly remained at the table and gazed out the window where night had fallen. Max would be snuggled in his bed at John's, without her nighttime kiss, without her being able to smell the little-boy scent, which wrapped around her heart.

For the first time in her life, Amberly found herself wondering if the job was worth the sacrifice. Surely anything that separated her from her son wasn't worth it. And yet working as an FBI agent was all she'd ever wanted to do.

And until this case, she'd always managed to juggle both the job and the son she loved quite well with John's help. This was the first time it had become complicated, and being away from Max was tearing her apart. She'd spoken to him only three times since leaving her house, all three times on a disposable phone that couldn't be traced, and hoping that somehow the killer wouldn't recognize that if he truly wanted to kill her, all he had to do was do something terrible to her son.

She got up from the table and walked into the living room and peered outside. Beneath the spill of a streetlight directly outside the house, she could see Roger Black's car parked.

At Cole's request, he was babysitting her until Cole got home. Who would have ever thought the time would come when she'd need a babysitter to assure her own safety?

She was supposed to be out there protecting others, not utilizing what little workforce there was in Mystic Lake to protect her. Frustration gnawed inside her as her mind whirled with the facts that they knew so far about the murders.

Too little. They knew just too damned little for her to do her job as a profiler and get into the head of the killer. Certainly, he haunted her sleep. For the past week, since she'd moved in here with Cole, she'd suffered one sort of nightmare or another about the crimes almost every night. Thankfully, she'd managed to wake herself up before she'd screamed or yelled to draw Cole's attention.

She was vaguely surprised the killer hadn't made any personal contact with either her or Cole since leaving the things on her mailbox. If he was the publicity hound that she suspected, then it wouldn't be out of character for him to call either her or Cole. But so far that hadn't happened.

Thinking of the devil, she saw Cole's car coming down the street, and instantly a coil of tension twisted in her stomach. She'd become accustomed to the feeling because it whirled inside her each time Cole was around.

She didn't take it out and examine it too closely. She knew it was desire and she also knew it had no place in a murder investigation or in her life.

She was a single parent and a dedicated FBI agent and an ex-wife who didn't expect to find the kind of love that others seemed to possess.

Cole parked in the driveway and then walked to Roger's car, where he leaned into the passenger window and spoke to the man. Several moments later, Cole approached the house and Roger pulled away from the curb.

"Hmm, something smells good," he said as he walked in the front door and locked it behind him. "And here's a little surprise for you." He handed her a sack.

"Chicken and homemade baked macaroni and cheese and green beans," she said and then smiled as she pulled out a large bag of red licorice. "Thank you."

He returned her smile, his the tired smile of a man who had worked too many hours. "You're welcome, and dinner sounds great. Maybe I should send you home early more often."

"You'll probably quickly discover that I do better work in the field than I do in the kitchen," she replied.

Together they walked into the kitchen, where Amberly began to place the food on the table and Cole washed his hands at the sink.

"This looks terrific," he said as he sat at the table.

"The macaroni and cheese is a little burnt. Take yours from the center. I like the crunchy burnt part around the edges."

She felt sudden tears burn at her eyes as she thought of Max teasing her about her addiction to burnt crisps of macaroni.

She quickly stuffed back the emotion but apparently not fast enough.

Cole studied her face solemnly. "What's wrong?" he asked.

It worried her, how adept he'd become over the past week in reading her every mood. There was a growing intimacy between them that had nothing to do with sex or physical attraction. It was a connection of minds, a nebulous connection she'd never felt with anyone else before.

"I was just thinking about how Max teases me when I eat this," she said as she scooped around the edge of the pan for the most burnt pieces.

"I know how difficult this has been for you." His gaze was soft, his eyes so blue, and she knew if she looked there for too long, she'd lose it altogether.

"We just need to catch this bastard so I can get back home where I belong," she replied.

He nodded and for the next few minutes they ate in silence, but the longer the silence went on, the more certain Amberly became that he had something on his mind.

It was that intimacy thing again, the fact that they were somehow on the same page emotionally and seemed unnaturally attuned to each other's moods.

"Anything happen after I went home today?" she finally asked when they were almost finished eating and the silence had become downright awkward.

"Nothing worthwhile." He hesitated a moment and then continued, "Although Ben had an interesting theory about the case."

Amberly sat back in her chair and stared at him expectantly. "What kind of theory?"

"Why don't we clear off these dishes and make some coffee and take it into the living room and talk about it then," he countered.

This time, a new kind of tension welled up inside her as she wondered what Ben had come up with that made

Cole want to make her as comfortable as possible before he shared the information with her.

It took them only minutes to clear the table, and as the coffee brewed, Cole left the kitchen to change out of his uniform.

Amberly had changed out of her business attire the minute she'd gotten home, opting for a pair of jeans and a purple tank top with a gold embellishment on the front in the shape of a feather.

By the time she'd poured the coffee and carried the cups and her bag of licorice into the living room, he'd returned, clad in a pair of jean shorts and a white T-shirt that stretched provocatively across his broad shoulders and showcased his lean stomach.

They sat side by side on the sofa, their cups on the coffee table before them, and she looked at him expectantly. "So, tell me about Ben's theory."

"It's a bit out there," he cautioned her.

She smiled and grabbed a piece of licorice from the package. "So is our theory of the Three Stooges working together as serial killers, but right now, we have nothing but theories that are a bit out there." She bit into the licorice stick.

"Ben wondered if maybe John could be behind all this." The words fell flat and stark from his mouth.

She stared at him as if he'd suddenly spoken a foreign language, and the piece of licorice turned tasteless in her mouth. "John?" She swallowed hard to dislodge the bite of candy from her throat. "You mean my John?"

Cole nodded. "The one and only."

She tried to wrap her mind around his words. "Why...

what…why on earth would Ben even think such a thing?" she sputtered in confusion. Surely he couldn't be serious.

Cole reached out for his coffee cup and took a sip. When he placed the cup back on the table, he looked at her once again. "I know on the surface it sounds ridiculous, but just take a minute and think about it."

"I am thinking about it, and no matter how long I think, it's still definitely ridiculous," she exclaimed. "First of all, John doesn't have it in him to murder innocent women. He's an artist, for heaven's sake. He creates beauty, he doesn't destroy it. Second, what on earth would he hope to gain by doing such a terrible thing as killing women in a small town?"

"We both know that all kinds of people are capable of murder, even artists who paint pretty pictures," Cole chided.

Amberly pulled her braid over her shoulder and worried her fingers through the end of it. "I just don't understand. I can't make the connection between John and what's been happening here in Mystic Lake." She looked at him in confusion and with a pool of worry unsettled in her stomach.

Had they learned something after she'd left that day that somehow tied John to the murders? She couldn't imagine John having anything to do with any of this, and yet she couldn't help but remember a few times in their marriage when John had shown true rage. Those occasions had been rare but a bit frightening at the time.

Afterward, they'd usually joke about the artist's temperament, and John was always contrite. Just because he occasionally had a temper flare, that didn't mean he was a killer. Everyone lost it occasionally. She stared at Cole, needing him to explain this theory so she could dismiss it completely.

Cole leaned back against the sofa and released a sigh as he held her gaze. "You told me that John would be thrilled if you came back to him. You also said he hated what you did for a living. What if he orchestrated these murders knowing that you'd probably get the call to investigate because of the dream-catcher element? What if he masterminded it so that he would separate you from the person you love most in the world? Make you question what you're doing with your life?"

She continued to stare at him, a hard lump filling her chest. She certainly didn't believe that particular scenario, that John could be behind any of this, but there was no question that she'd been sitting at the kitchen table an hour earlier and questioning her commitment to the job.

But it was crazy, wasn't it? It was just a crazy theory that had nothing to do with reality.

To her surprise, Cole reached out and covered one of her hands with his, the simple contact helping to warm all the places that had grown cold with the conversation.

"I was doubting the job a little while ago," she admitted. "I was wondering about the choices I've made, if I was crazy to want to do this job, knowing that in this particular case, it got too close to home, too close to Max."

"You're good at what you do, Amberly. It would be a damn shame if you decided to give it all up. We need people like you doing what you do, otherwise the bad guys win. There are plenty of people who have it all, the family and the job." His eyes darkened. "And most of the time, it works out okay."

This from a man who had lost his wife to a murderer, this from a man who had been robbed of the woman he loved because the job had gotten tangled up with his personal life.

"How do you go on when something happens like losing your loved one?" she asked softly. "How did you get through it?"

His hand embraced hers, their fingers locking together as he held her gaze intently. "You get through it one minute at a time. You grieve long and deep, you bury yourself in it, and then one day you wake up and realize life is still going on. The sun is rising in the mornings and it sets every evening and you have a choice to either participate in life or kill yourself. I knew Emily loved me enough to want me to go on, and lately I've realized that she would want me to go on and find happiness wherever I could, that she wouldn't want me to live the rest of my life alone."

"It must be horrible," she said.

"It was, but as Granny Nightsong would say, at some point you have to reach acceptance, otherwise it's like a tick in your armpit, sucking the life out of you."

She knew he'd hoped to coax a smile from her by quoting Granny's words back at her, but she was still too focused on the idea of John being a suspect.

"John didn't do this," she replied, not wanting to think about Cole's loss or contemplate the potential of any loss of her own.

"Probably not, but I have to tell you I'm going to investigate him."

"It's going to be a waste of your time." She wasn't sure whether to be angry at this turn of events, defensive of the man she'd loved as a friend and mistakenly married, or simply sad that their investigaten had derailed so far off course.

"I'm sorry, Amberly," Cole said, pulling her back from her thoughts. "But now that it's in my head, I can't just dismiss it."

She sighed. "I know you have to do your job, and I know that this is one part of the investigation I can't participate in." If this particular leg of the investigation was somehow screwed up and she was involved, it would be easy to prove bias on her part. "I had no idea when I arrived here on that first day that things were going to get so complicated."

He smiled, that soft smile that melted any hardness she might possess inside her heart. "I never dreamed on that first day that I'd have the slightly arrogant FBI agent right here in my house, wearing a tank top that's totally distracting and seated close enough for me to kiss."

Her heart stopped beating at his words. Somehow they had gone from a difficult conversation and veered into something that felt as dangerous as anything she'd ever experienced before.

A million thoughts flew through her head, a million reasons why they shouldn't explore this new territory. And yet, the thought of being in Cole's arms, of having his mouth on hers was not only a welcome escape from her concerns about John and the case, but also felt as if it had been an itch that needed to be scratched since the minute she had met him.

"Then why don't you kiss me," she replied as her heart trembled and she leaned forward ever so slightly.

As COLE LEANED FORWARD and claimed Amberly's lips, he knew he was starting something he desperately wanted to finish. But he had no idea what her intentions were as she opened her mouth to welcome his kiss.

All thoughts of murder, of mental and physical exhaustion fled as he quickly became intoxicated with the taste of her, with the exotic floral scent of her that wrapped around him.

It had been years since he'd wanted a woman the way he now wanted Amberly. As she wound her arms around his neck and pulled herself more closely against him, he knew this wasn't going to stop with just a kiss.

He could taste the desire, could feel the tension inside her, a tension that had been building to mammoth proportions since the moment she'd moved in here. There was no way there wasn't going to be an explosion, and he felt the beginning simmer of one now.

"You know we'd be fools to let this go any further," she whispered when their lips finally parted.

"There are times that being a fool isn't necessarily a bad thing," he replied. He pulled the end of her braid forward and worked to remove the rubber band at the end. He wanted that rich darkness loose and flowing. He needed to tangle his hands in the thickness of that dark curtain of hair.

She sat perfectly still as he carefully unwound the

braid, but he could sense her quickened heartbeat as her eyes darkened. As the braid uncoiled into shiny, wavy lengths, he felt as if they were indulging in a form of foreplay.

He was already fully aroused, and all he'd done was kiss her and toy with her hair. He stroked her hair and then placed a lingering kiss on the side of her neck.

"Maybe we should take this into your bedroom," she said, her voice half-breathless.

His heartbeat accelerated as he realized she was as into the moment, as into him as he was into her. "That sounds like a great idea." He got up from the sofa and held out his hand to her.

She hesitated for a beat, and he feared she might change her mind, and he felt that if he didn't have her now, this moment would never come again.

He breathed an inward sigh of relief as she slipped her hand into his and stood. They walked down the hallway in silence, but he wondered if she could hear the frantic pounding of his heart.

When they reached his bedroom, he gathered her back into his arms, reveling in the warmth of her curves against him. Once again his mouth found hers in a fiery kiss that left no question as to what was about to happen between them.

He slid his hands up beneath the tank top she wore, her skin soft and warm to his touch. She leaned closer to him, her hips molding to his, and he knew there was no way she couldn't tell that he was ready for her.

With an adeptness he had forgotten he possessed, he unfastened her bra with a flick of his fingers. She stepped back from him only long enough to pull the tank top over her head and allow her bra to fall to the floor in front of her.

As she did that, he pulled off his T-shirt, wanting to feel her full, naked breasts against his bare chest. They came back together and once again kissed with passion, with all the desire that had simmered for what felt like an entire lifetime.

There was no thought of tomorrow, no thought of what might come next; he was completely lost in the moment, lost in Amberly.

It didn't take long for them to get undressed and in the bed. Cole stroked his fingers across her high cheekbones, along the smooth skin of her cheek and over the full lips that so tormented him.

"You are so beautiful," he said softly.

"You're just saying that because I'm naked in your bed," she replied with a husky voice.

He laughed. "No, it's more than physical. You have a beautiful mind, Amberly. You draw me to you." He wanted to tell her that he hadn't felt this way about anyone since his wife, but he was afraid of what her reaction might be.

She'd made it clear to him that she wasn't looking for a relationship. This night was an unexpected gift, and he didn't want to frighten her away by making it a bigger deal than she wanted...needed...it to be.

"I want you, Cole." Her eyes glowed in the light spilling into the bedroom from the hallway. "I've never felt this kind of want before. It scares me just a little."

"Don't be scared." He wanted her to embrace her

desire for him, to wallow in it, in him as he intended to do in her. With this thought in mind, he stopped the conversation by kissing her as he began to explore her body in earnest.

Despite his own need, his first thought was to give her the greatest experience she'd ever had in a bedroom. He quickly learned that kissing her along her slender throat caused her to mewl but teasing the tips of her breasts made her clench the sheet at her sides and moan with pleasure.

As he slid his hand down the flat of her stomach, he felt her catch her breath in anticipation. Her entire body seemed to vibrate as he slipped his hand between her legs, finding the moist warmth. A gasp escaped her lips.

As he moved his fingers against the sensitive spot, she tensed and whispered his name. When he quickened his caresses, she cried his name and clutched his shoulders in a tight grasp.

He felt the climax that shuddered through her, and a wild euphoria filled him. But they weren't finished yet. He gave her a moment to catch her breath and then moved between her thighs. As he hovered over her, her eyes flared, and her hands moved from his shoulders to his buttocks.

"I want you inside me," she said, and he wouldn't have believed she could say anything that would drive his desire higher, but that did.

Until this moment he'd maintained complete control of their lovemaking, but as he eased into her dampness, he felt his control snap.

He hissed in pleasure as he buried himself deep inside

her, for a moment not moving, just being connected in the most intimate way a man could connect with a woman. Closing his eyes, he felt surrounded, engulfed and possessed by Amberly.

It was she who snapped him out of the moment, moving her hips against his. He opened his eyes and looked down into hers as they began to move together in unison.

He saw the wonder in her eyes as their movements increased, becoming faster, a tad bit frantic. He felt himself getting lost in the need for release and yet wanted her to join him.

And then he knew that she was there with him, hanging on the precipice of another climax. He cried out her name and tangled his hands in her hair as he felt his release and, at the same time, felt her stiffen and shudder and knew that she had found her own.

For long moments afterward, they remained in each other's embrace, trying to catch their runaway breaths. When he finally had his wind back, he released a low rumble of laughter.

"I don't know about you, but I needed that…I needed you," he said.

She smiled, a languid gesture that spoke of utter contentment. "I hate to confess that I've wanted this… wanted you…since the minute I laid eyes on you." Her smile faded. "But this certainly didn't move us any closer to solving the case, and it's probably just complicated things between the two of us."

He frowned. "Complicate things how?"

A tiny smile danced across her features once again.

"Because now that I realize how very well you do this, I just might want to do it again."

"And I would have a problem with that, why?" he asked wryly.

"Because I think maybe you're ready for something more in your life than me." She moved out of his arms and sat up and worried a hand through her long hair. "Whatever this is that we're feeling, it's just a fleeting thing…lust and nothing more. I'm here to do a job, and all this can be with us is a fringe benefit."

She slid from the bed and padded naked into his bathroom and closed the door behind her. Cole folded his arms behind his head and stared up at the ceiling.

The euphoria he'd experienced only moments before had vanished, squashed beneath a sudden weight of depression.

How had this happened? How was it that he had three murder cases he wasn't closer to solving than the day the bodies had been discovered and a potential victim living beneath his roof?

Still, what bothered him at the moment was the fact that he was precariously close to falling in love with a woman who'd made it clear that romance and marriage had no place in her life.

## Chapter Ten

Amberly paced the floor of the conference room, occasionally stopping in front of the bulletin board to stare blankly at the crime-scene photos, but her thoughts weren't on the crimes. Her head was consumed with thoughts of Cole.

He'd left earlier with Ben to drive to Kansas City and question John. She was anxious to hear what they'd discovered when they returned, although she was certain there was nothing to discover.

As anxious as she was about their investigation of John, she was equally confused and still a little flustered by her lovemaking with Cole.

Nothing in her marriage had prepared her for what had happened between herself and Cole in his bed the night before. The passion she'd always feared she'd never experience had exploded out of her in Cole's arms, and it had been sheer, unadulterated passion for him.

Lust, she tried to tell herself. And everyone knew that lust didn't last, that it eventually waned and left nothing behind. That hadn't been her problem in her marriage. There had never been any lust for her where John was concerned, just a bottle of champagne and a night of mistakes.

Had last night with Cole been a mistake? How could she possibly categorize that splendid act as a mistake? She hadn't known how wonderful lovemaking could be until last night. And now she would never want to settle for anything less.

He was getting to her, with his blue eyes and hot body. But more than that, he was getting to her with his compassion, with his intelligence and with his very heart, and she couldn't allow that to happen.

Her life was complicated without a man in it. She had Max to consider, and she'd absolutely made a vow to herself when she'd divorced that she wouldn't drag a parade of men through his life.

At least she hadn't slept in Cole's bed. After they'd made love, she'd gone back to the guest room, afraid that by sleeping in his arms, by awakening with him in the same bed to the morning light, what they'd shared would somehow transform into something deeper than mere lust.

She needed to be home. There had been no other threats against her since the photo and dream catcher hung on her mailbox. Maybe they'd jumped the gun by removing her from her home, from her son.

Sure, there was no question that the message sent to her mailbox had frightened her, but maybe it had been nothing more than a prank played by one of the men she'd fooled the night she'd gone to the bar and hadn't told anyone she was an FBI agent.

She stared back at the crime-scene photos, her heart

beating an uneven rhythm as she gazed at the victims. Was she willing to take a chance with her life, assume that it had been just a prank? Was she willing to take a chance on Max's life?

She turned away from the board as Roger Black entered the room. "Thought you might like some lunch," the deputy said as he placed a fast-food bag on the table.

"Lunch? Already?" She looked at her watch and realized it was just after twelve. Where had the morning gone? "Thanks, Roger. It was really sweet of you to think of me. What do I owe you?"

His cheeks blushed a bit. "Don't worry about it, it's just a cheeseburger and fries." He headed for the door. "I'll get you one of those diet drinks you like from the vending machine."

Before she could protest, he was out of the room. She sank down on the table and opened the bag. He'd ordered her cheeseburger just the way she liked them, with no onions and double cheese.

It was just another indication that she'd been in Mystic Lake for too long. Everyone knew how she ordered her burgers, what she liked to drink, and the small police force had been as accommodating to her as anyone could be.

She smiled as Roger returned to the room, her diet drink in one hand and a canned orange in the other. "Here you go." He set her drink in front of her and then sat across the table. "How're you doing?"

"Hanging in there," she replied as she plucked a hot fry out of the paper container. "Although it seems to be taking Ben and Cole an unusual amount of time to question John."

"I know they wanted to find a time when your little guy wasn't around, and you know how these things go… it always takes longer to interview somebody than you think it's going to take."

She offered him some of her fries but he shook his head. She took another one, ate it and then focused back on Roger. "What do you think about all this? You have a specific theory to the case?"

"I still think Jeff Maynard is good for the murders. He's a nasty piece of work. It's easy for me to imagine him killing Gretchen and getting off on the power of the kill."

"Enough to make him kill again and again?"

Roger nodded. "I just think he's the type that once he got the taste of murder in his mouth, he liked it. Besides, it would tickle him to death to sit back and watch us run around like chickens with our heads missing."

"What about the dream catchers?" she asked and then bit into her cheeseburger.

Roger frowned. "That's the part I just can't make sense of, no matter how I twist it around in my mind." Roger snaked one of her fries out of the container and then popped the top of his soda. "I can't imagine that Jeff would know a dream catcher from a tom-tom drum."

"And I can't imagine my ex-husband had anything to do with any of this," Amberly said, tension tightening in her chest.

"I think Cole was looking to definitively count him out rather than seriously looking at him as a suspect."

Roger's words released some of the tension. "I hope you're right." She glanced at her wristwatch. "And I wish they'd get back here soon. The waiting to hear how it went is about to kill me."

As if conjured up by her very wishes, at that moment, Cole and Ben entered the room.

"It's about time," she said, her appetite gone as she stared first at Ben and then at Cole. "So, what happened?"

"We didn't get any real definite answers as far as alibis for the nights of the murders," Ben said.

"According to John, many evenings when he's alone, he shuts off his phone and works. He says his best creativity happens late in the night or in the very early morning hours. Apparently, the last month he's been working overtime to get paintings ready for a show he has coming up," Cole said.

Amberly nodded. "That's right. He has a big show scheduled, and he does often work late into the night all alone." During the years they'd been married, John had often started painting after dinner and had worked into the wee hours of the morning.

"Makes it tough to confirm an alibi." Cole sank down at the table in a nearby chair. "Although he did think that on one of those nights he'd played chess with your neighbor, Ed."

"And so we stopped at Ed's and spoke to him," Ben said. "He wasn't good at particular dates, but said he and John frequently play chess in the evenings."

"That's true," Amberly replied. She fought against a sigh of frustration. "So, is he still a suspect, or did he answer your questions satisfactorily enough that we can mark him off our short list?"

"I'm still ambivalent," Cole confessed after a moment of hesitation.

Deep disappointment flared through Amberly. She'd hoped to at least have some closure where this situation was concerned. Her heart rebelled at the very thought that the man she'd married, the man who had been her best friend for the past eight years, could actually be a monster.

But there was no question that since Cole had told her Ben's crazy theory she was having trouble completely dismissing it from her mind.

"So, what happens now?" she asked.

"I think we all go back to the drawing board," Cole said, his gaze moving to the pictures of the victims. "Somehow we've missed something, a key piece that would point a finger at somebody."

"It's the dream catcher," Amberly said without hesitation. "Until we figure out what meaning it has to our killer, we won't have the clue we really need."

Cole frowned thoughtfully. "We need to delve deeper into the suspects we have and, at the same time, reinterview family members and friends of both the suspects and victims. I'm afraid we're back into the drudgery of leg- and paperwork."

Ben smiled easily. "And unlike what is seen on television, that's usually what solves crimes."

"What we're looking for is either Native American ties or specific affinities to dream catchers," Cole said.

He appointed a victim and a suspect to each deputy and kept Jeff to reinvestigate for himself.

He assigned Amberly nothing, and she figured it was because he identified her as a potential victim and didn't want her running off on her own to investigate anything.

After the two deputies had left the room, Cole moved to sit next to Amberly. "I wish I had the words to erase those worry lines that are creasing your brow," he said.

"The only thing that will do that is getting this creep behind bars and letting me go home to Max." What she wanted to do was melt into his arms, for him to hold her and tell her that everything was going to be okay.

The victims cried out for justice, and she just wanted to hold her son close and assure herself that he was happy and healthy. "Do you really think I'm in some kind of danger?" she asked.

This time, it was Cole's forehead that wrinkled with worry lines. "I don't know," he admitted. "I expected another body or something to happen before now. I thought he was escalating, but I think maybe he's just cunning and calculating, waiting for the best possible opportunity to strike again."

"If I've been marked as his next victim, maybe he didn't anticipate that I'd move out and come here to stay with you. Maybe that slowed down his time line a bit."

"Perhaps. But I don't know why he hasn't just picked another victim. Even though I've warned the young women in this town not to be out alone, that doesn't mean they're all heeding the warning." Cole stood abruptly. "Come on, let's go see what we can find out about Jeff

Maynard's past. Somehow, the answer is here in town. We just need to find it."

"Then let's get to it," she replied.

For the next five hours, she and Cole talked to everyone who knew Jeff Maynard. They asked about any Native American he might have in his background, if he'd ever shown or talked about any interest in Native American history or myths and legends.

"I'd like to get a warrant and search wherever he's been staying, maybe get hold of a computer he uses," Cole said once they were back at the office.

"Unfortunately, a judge wouldn't even entertain the notion of a search warrant based on what we have," she replied. "We have a public fight between him and Gretchen, but he also has an alibi we haven't been able to break for the time of her murder."

Cole checked his watch. "It's after seven. I guess we'll call it a day and head home."

Minutes later, as they rode back to his house, Amberly felt his discouragement. "You know, the FBI doesn't always get it right, and some crimes are never solved," she said softly.

"Don't even think that," he replied firmly. "We're going to find this guy and stop him. I won't quit until I've found him."

"I like a man with that kind of determination," she said in an attempt to lighten the mood.

"What kind of food would you like for dinner? Personally, unless you're in the mood to cook I'm all in for takeout."

"Is there a Chinese place somewhere? I'm definitely a fool for sweet-and-sour chicken," she said.

"Mr. Wok's, two blocks away. I just like eating out of cartons with chopsticks."

She laughed, although it certainly wasn't a laugh from her heart. They were both making light to cast away the discouragement over the fact that they couldn't catch a break to nail the killer.

Thirty minutes later, the two of them were seated at Cole's kitchen table eating from half a dozen different cartons from Mr. Wok's.

"What worries me is that the break we're waiting for will come at the price of somebody else's life," she said as she speared a piece of sweet-and-sour chicken with the end of a chopstick.

"That worries me, too." Cole leaned back in his chair and shoved his empty plate away. "Even in the years I worked in St. Louis, I never had a case where there was no significant evidence left behind. Whoever is doing this has to be smart and very organized."

"And that takes our top three suspects right off the list," she said dryly.

He returned her smile. "I'd be the first to admit that I don't believe Jeff, Raymond or Jimmy are the sharpest crayons in the box, but I also don't want to underestimate any of them. One of them might just be playing the fool."

Amberly ate the last piece of chicken off her plate and then leaned back in her chair. "How long do we do this? How long do I keep away from Max? From my life?"

"I wish I had an answer for you, but I don't. All I know is that I feel like something is going to break soon, that whoever is committing these crimes won't be able to help himself from committing another one very soon."

"I feel it, too," Amberly admitted. "It's like the tick of a time bomb that's been hidden in the room, but no matter how hard we search we can't find the bomb, and detonation is about to happen." A shiver worked up her spine, and she wrapped her arms around herself in an attempt to stave it off.

Cole reached across the table and covered one of her hands with his. "I've only felt this helpless one other time in my entire life, and that was when I couldn't get to my wife in time to save her. If this creep's intention is to get to you, then I just want you to know that he'll have to come through me to do it." There was a fierce protectiveness to his tone that she found oddly comforting.

She curled her fingers with his. "Thanks, but it's not me I'm worried about."

"Max?" he asked. "John won't let anything happen to him."

"I know that. Even if I believed that John was capable of the murders of these women, I know he'd never hurt Max." She paused, a tightness filling her chest. "I just keep having that same bad dream about him. He's running all alone in the dark. He's so afraid and he's lost his protection charm and I can't get to him."

Cole's eyes were soft blue depths as he held her gaze. "Why don't you sleep with me tonight in my bed, let me be your own personal dream catcher," he said. "Sleep in my arms, and let me keep your bad dreams away."

Amberly knew if she accepted his offer, they'd probably wind up making love again. She also knew there was nothing that she'd love more than to sleep dreamlessly in his strong, safe arms.

She didn't want to think about whether it was right or wrong, she didn't want to consider any consequences, she just wanted to feel his body next to hers, his heartbeat against her own.

She was suddenly overwhelmed with a bone-weary exhaustion, with the grief of missing Max and with the need to allow not just any man but Cole Caldwell to take control of her, to wrap her in his arms and steal any bad dreams out of her head.

"Yes, please," she said simply.

COLE AWAKENED BEFORE dawn, Amberly snuggled against his side and sound asleep. They'd left Mr. Wok's on the table the night before and had undressed and tumbled into his bed.

Silently, they had made love, and it had been afterward, when she curled up in his arms and fell asleep, that he realized he was in love with her.

He hadn't been looking for it, certainly hadn't wanted to feel these kinds of feelings and emotions again in his lifetime, but they were there nevertheless, and there was nothing he could do about them. He certainly had no intention of letting her know how he felt.

He knew from the conversations they'd had in the past week that she felt guilty about leaving John, that she hated the fact that John was in love with her and she didn't, couldn't love him back.

The last thing Cole would do was burden her with his

love for her. She'd made it clear that she wasn't ready for a new man in her life, didn't believe in love that lasted.

All he needed to do was stay focused on solving the murders so she could get back to her life with her son. That would be the best gift he could give her.

He closed his eyes although he knew any further sleep would be impossible. He should get up and look at the files again, see what they'd missed, if they'd missed anything vital, but he was reluctant to leave the bed and Amberly.

He found it difficult to take Ben's theory of John being guilty of the crimes too seriously. When he'd talked to John, the artist had appeared completely forthcoming despite the fact that he didn't have any really solid alibis for the nights of the murders.

It was obvious that John was still hung up on Amberly and that he loved both her and his son to distraction, but John seemed too smart to be the killer. He'd have to know that the dream catchers would point to Amberly and ultimately come back on him. Hell, with John making his living painting Western art, he'd probably painted more than one dream catcher in his career.

Cole frowned, his eyes still closed. Still, as much as he wanted to completely dismiss John Merriweather from the suspect list, he couldn't. As he'd told Amberly, he was ambivalent about the man.

It all came back to the dream catchers. They felt like a personal call to action for Amberly. Maybe instead of the key to the crimes being the dream catchers, maybe Amberly was really the key.

He remained in bed until dawn began to light the sky

and seep in through his window, and only then did he slide out, leaving Amberly still asleep.

He grabbed a clean uniform and went to the hall bathroom to shower and dress, and once that was done, he went into the kitchen to make a pot of coffee.

Minutes later, he stood at the window and sipped a cup of the fresh brew, his mind whirling with new thoughts. They'd investigated the victims to find a pattern, they'd interrogated the men they thought might be capable of murder, but nobody had thought to interrogate one of the investigators of the crimes.

He felt energized by the new trail that had suddenly opened up to him. All he had to do was wait until Amberly got up to ask her some questions about past cases she had worked on or enemies she might have made.

It was possible that Mystic Lake was just the random small town close to Kansas City where the killer had decided to play his games, games that were intended specifically to draw Amberly in.

He should have known it was personally directed at her when the dream catcher and photo had been hung on her mailbox. He'd just assumed somebody had followed her home from Mystic Lake, but it was possible their perp was closer to her home than to his.

He was on his second cup of coffee when she finally came into the kitchen. She'd showered and was dressed in her black slacks and a white blouse. Her hair was neatly braided, and she looked more rested than she had all week.

"Good morning," she said with a bright smile as she beelined to the coffeemaker on the countertop.

"You slept well?" he asked although he already knew the answer.

"Like a baby," she replied. She poured herself a cup of coffee and sat in a chair at the table.

He refilled his cup and then sat in the chair opposite hers. "I've been thinking," he began.

"Uh-oh," she said and quickly took a sip from her mug. "I'm not sure I like the sound of that."

"I've been thinking that maybe we've been approaching all of this from the wrong angle."

She cocked her head and frowned. "What do you mean?"

"I kept thinking that the key to the murders somehow rested with the dream catchers that were left at the scenes."

She nodded and took another drink of coffee. "We've both been functioning with that thought in mind."

"I think we've been wrong. I think the dream catchers were just a ploy and the real key to the killer is you."

Her dark eyes widened slightly. "Are we talking about John again?"

"Not necessarily. But I think the killer is somebody from your life, somebody who is just using Mystic Lake as his playground, and the victims and the dream catchers were just a ploy to get you here. I think Ben was right as far as that part of his theory. I don't know if it's John or not, but you need to think about other cases you've been involved in, people you've had fights with and anyone who would want to hurt you. I want you to take Mystic Creek out of the mix and anyone else but you."

She sat back in her chair and wrapped her fingers around her mug, as if his words had suddenly made her hands go cold. "I can't imagine anyone who would go to these lengths to hurt me," she said after a moment of hesitation. "The last case I worked was a kidnapping for ransom, but I wasn't lead on the case and didn't have that much interaction with the perp who was caught." She shook her head, obviously at a loss. "I try not to make enemies in my life. Granny Nightsong always taught me to tread lightly and leave no footprints behind."

"A nice concept but almost impossible to do." He took a sip of his coffee and then placed the mug back on the table and leaned forward.

"Sometimes you step on toes and don't even realize it at the time. You're tired and frustrated and snap at somebody who doesn't deserve your attitude. There's got to be somebody, Amberly, and we need to start someplace with this new theory."

"So, what do you need from me?"

"I'd like you to make a list of coworkers who might not be thrilled with you. I want you to write down the names of neighbors and friends you interact with on a regular basis, criminals who might have a personal reason to hate you."

"You really believe this is somebody from my life and not just some creep from your town?"

"I can't be sure. But we've been spinning our wheels in my town. Now I think we need to spend some time spinning them in your life." He could tell by the darkness of her eyes how much the idea disturbed her.

"You still think John might be responsible for all this."

It wasn't a question but rather a flat statement that held the undertone of displeasure.

"Do you really think I'd park my son with a man I thought was capable of killing anyone? I've known John for almost eight years, was married to him for three of those years." She moved her hands from her mug as she continued. "I'm not a stupid woman, I'm an FBI agent, and I would have seen through the years, I would have sensed, if something was this off with John."

"I'm definitely leaning toward the assumption of John's innocence," Cole said softly. "But I'm also leaning toward this being all about you and the fact that Mystic Lake is involved at all might be incidental."

"I think I liked it better when it was some crazy serial killer just randomly murdering women," she replied.

"It's still that," he countered. "I just think whoever it is wanted you specifically on this case, wanted you away from your comfort zone because it might make you a more vulnerable victim."

She rubbed two fingers across her forehead as if to ease a headache that had begun to pound.

"I'm sorry," he said. "I should have at least waited to talk to you about this until you'd had your second cup of coffee."

She flashed him a quick smile that warmed him from head to toe. "I'm not sure that an entire pot of coffee would have managed to take the sting out of this conversation."

"At this point, it's just another crazy theory," he said in an attempt to take away the sting. "For the moment, we remove John from the scenario and see who else you might come up with." He got up from his chair. "And now I'm going to make us some breakfast so we can start the day off right."

"A little late for that," she muttered.

Still, by the time they'd eaten eggs and toast and sausage links and she'd downed another two cups of coffee, she appeared ready to focus on this new task.

"Are there any more Native American agents in the Kansas City office?" he asked as they drove to the office.

"No, I'm the token Injun," she said, deliberately being politically incorrect.

"So, it would be natural for somebody to believe that the dream catchers at the sites might encourage the FBI to call you in."

"There's nothing about any of this that's natural," she replied. "But yes, I suppose that makes a certain kind of crazy sense."

"Do you have other Native American friends? Somebody who maybe has a beef with you, somebody for whom the dream catcher might mean something personal?"

She shook her head. "There's a Native American center in Kansas City, but I've never been there. I know a couple of men who work there, but they're good men."

"Everyone, I want everyone on the list you're going to make," Cole said firmly. "I don't care if you believe they're good men or not. If this is really all about you, then we need to know about everyone in your life."

By that time, they'd reached the office, where, for the next hour, Amberly sat in the conference room with a legal pad and a pen in front of her and listened while Cole discussed his newest theory with the other deputies.

She looked fragile as if, for the first time since finding the items on her mailbox, the full realization of the danger she was in from somebody who might be close to her had finally struck.

He wanted nothing more than to pull her into his arms, shield her from anything that made her eyes darken with fear and her lips to quiver with emotion.

He wanted to fix her world, even knowing that once it was fixed she'd go back to her life and he'd once again be alone, only this time he'd be alone with a bruised and battered heart.

"I'll check in with you around noon," he said to her after the deputies had left the room. "You'll be okay here?"

She looked down at the blank legal pad in front of her. "Sure, just me and all the people who might want me dead." She reached into her purse and pulled out the bag of licorice he'd bought her the night before. "I'll be fine. Go do some sheriffing."

He fought the impulse to lean forward and kiss her on the forehead. Instead, he left the office and hit the streets. It was cooler today, feeling more like autumn than the late-summer weather they'd enjoyed until now. The skies were overcast, and Cole found his mood reflecting the dreariness of the day.

He'd forgotten what it felt like to be in love, and while it filled his soul with joy, he knew it wasn't what Amberly wanted or needed in her life. All she needed from him was to solve this crime and send her back home, and it was the one thing he had yet to be able to do for her.

Although he'd downplayed to her his feelings about John's guilt, he still felt as if her ex-husband had the most to gain from this particular case. John knew Native American culture. He'd also probably known that Amberly was the only Native American working out of the Kansas City office.

But he was willing to admit that it might be somebody else altogether, somebody with a grudge against Amberly, and only she could identify that person for them.

He just hoped she could do it soon, for he definitely felt the tick of that time bomb, and if it exploded, he somehow feared she might not survive the blast.

## Chapter Eleven

At lunchtime, Amberly grabbed a sandwich and soda from the vending machine in the break room and then returned to the conference room and the list that wasn't happening.

The only name she could come up with was John, and her heart continued to rebel at the very idea that he could be behind all this with the notion of somehow forcing her back into his arms, back into his life.

By four, she'd managed to add three more names to her list, one of the men who worked at the Native American Center, who had expressed dissatisfaction over the fact that she wasn't involved in any way with the facility. A second name was a female coworker who had never hidden the fact that she thought Amberly had progressed in her career solely on the fact that she was a minority. Finally, she'd written down John's brother's name. Although he lived in a suburb of Kansas City and had rarely visited them, he'd made it clear that he wasn't a fan of Amberly's.

She didn't believe any of the people on her list were responsible for the crimes. She didn't know why those women had been killed or what the dream catchers really meant.

She felt so out of her element with this particular case. No matter how she twisted the pieces, she couldn't make them fit into a comprehensive picture. She absolutely couldn't get into the head of the killer, and that's what she was supposed to do well.

With a sigh of frustration, she dropped her head onto the cradle of her arms on the table, and instantly her thoughts turned to Cole and the night before.

She'd known it would be a mistake to get into his bed. She'd known they would make love again and they had, and it had been just as magical as the first time.

Apparently he had been her dream catcher, for she'd slept without dreams, snuggled against his warmth and listening to the strong, steady beat of his heart.

He could almost make her believe in love that lasted forever, in passion that never waned. What he couldn't do was take her back in time and meet her before she met John, before she had Max, before it all got so complicated.

Besides, she wouldn't want to go back in time because then she wouldn't have had Max, and that little guy awed her with his heart, with his head and with his very existence in her world.

Tears burned at her eyes as she thought of her son. Her need to hold him, to smell him, was nearly overwhelming. Her very womb ached as if he'd been violently ripped away from her.

She needed to be home with Max. That was her world,

that was her life, but she couldn't. She was too afraid of bringing danger with her.

And this thing with Cole, this magic she felt when she was with him, she had to forget it. She'd sworn that Max's life would come before hers, that she'd wait until he was older before even thinking about bringing a new man around him. The last thing she wanted to do was confuse him.

She raised her head as Roger came into the room. "What's up?" she asked.

"Nothing. Absolutely nothing." He sat across from her and gestured toward her legal pad. "Doesn't look like much is happening there, either."

She smiled at the young deputy. "What can I tell you? I try not to make enemies."

He returned her smile. "I could write down the names of at least four people I've pissed off just today."

His smile faded as he stared at the photos on the bulletin board. "Maybe it's somebody who is angry at your husband, maybe somebody who bought a painting of a dream catcher from him. I looked up some of his work online, and in his early years, he painted a whole series of dream catchers."

Amberly frowned and reached for a piece of licorice and then offered the bag to Roger, who shook his head negatively. "So this might all be about somebody who thinks they paid too much for a John Merriweather painting, and instead of asking for their money back, they decide to kill innocent women and lure me to this little town so they can kill me, too?"

She shook her head and bit into the licorice, hoping

the candy would help ease the headache she'd been fighting off all day.

"No matter how I twist and turn things, I can't make anything fit," she finally said.

"We all feel the same way," Roger replied. "We've never had crimes like this in Mystic Lake, but we're all doing the best we can to solve them." There was a touch of defensiveness in his voice.

"You all are a great team, and Cole is a terrific, smart sheriff. I'm certainly not dogging the team. I just can't believe that none of us can get a break that might lead us toward solving these murders."

"It's not from lack of trying. I've never worked the kind of hours I have in the last month."

She nodded. "I've only been here a short time, and I already feel about half burnt out."

"Sheriff thinks something is going to happen any day now. He thinks the killer won't be able to control himself much longer. He's deputized a couple of extra men to do night patrols around town."

Cole hadn't told her about it, but it didn't surprise her. She knew his biggest worry at the moment was that somehow the killer would get to her, or take another of the young women in the town he considered his own.

It was almost five when Cole came into the room, and instantly Amberly's heart lifted at the sight of him. When had it happened? When had the mere sight of him caused butterflies in her stomach to dance happily? When had the sound of his voice made her feel so safe despite any danger that might lurk nearby?

"Hi," he said to both her and Roger, although the warmth of his eyes lingered on her. "How are we doing?"

"My list is pathetic," Amberly confessed as she shoved the legal pad toward Cole.

He picked it up and looked at it. "You really don't make many enemies, do you?"

"Granny Nightsong always told me that my moccasins should never leave footprints of anger behind me," she replied. "And I've tried to live my life with that in mind."

"It would be a hell of a lot easier on all of us if you had some real enemies," Roger replied with a rueful grin.

At that moment, Amberly's cell phone rang. With a frown, she dug it out of her purse. She'd had few calls in the past week, and when she saw John's number on the caller identification, her heart gave a little lurch of anxiety.

"John?" she said.

A low, deep moan filled the line and panic stabbed through her. "John, is that you?" She jumped up from the table, her heart pounding so fast she felt like she might throw up.

There was another moan and then silence.

"John! John!" she yelled, but there was no response, just the ongoing silence, which chilled her to the bone. "Something's happened at John's house," she said to Cole as she hung up her phone. "We've got to get there right away. It sounded like he was hurt."

"Call it in to the Kansas City police," he instructed Roger and quickly gave him John's address. Then within seconds, he and Amberly were out the door and on the highway with sirens blaring and lights swirling.

Amberly's heart continued to rap a rhythm that was near heart-attack pace as she tried over and over again to call John back, but her calls kept going to his voice mail.

"Why doesn't he answer? What could be wrong?" She heard the hysteria in her voice but had no control over it. She couldn't even mention the question that pounded in her head. Where was Max? He should be there with John. So, why hadn't Max picked up his father's phone?

If something terrible had happened to John, then where in the name of God was Max? Everything faded away except the cell phone buttons she continued to punch and the fear that exploded in every molecule of her being.

She turned to Cole and saw his lips moving, but she couldn't hear him. She was trapped in a void of terror where no sound could get in, where nothing mattered except getting to John's as quickly as possible.

The drive from Mystic Lake to Kansas City seemed to take forever. With each mile, every minute that passed, Amberly's emotions rose to greater heights, threatening the loss of complete control.

As they pulled onto the street where John lived, her heart nearly stopped beating as she saw several police cars and an ambulance in the driveway.

She was out of the car before Cole's vehicle had come to a full stop. The dying grass rasped beneath her shoes as she raced across it toward the front door of the house. "John? Max?"

A police officer stopped her at the door. Holding back a sob of apprehension, she fumbled to show him her credentials. "I'm his ex-wife. Where is my son?"

She looked past the officer and saw John seated on the sofa. A couple of paramedics were working on the back of his head, and he looked dazed and half-conscious.

She shoved past the officer and fell to her knees in front of her ex-husband. "John…what happened? Where's Max?"

He stared at her as if he'd never seen her before. "I just answered the door. He hit me in the head with something."

"Who?"

"I don't know. He had on a ski mask." John wobbled, and his eyes drifted shut.

"John! Where's Max?" she asked urgently.

"We've got to get this man to the hospital," one of the paramedics said, and at the same time, an officer pulled Amberly to her feet and away from John.

She turned to him. "My son. Do you know where my son is?"

She was vaguely aware of Cole stepping up next to her and quickly introducing himself.

"Ma'am, there was no child here when we arrived. We found your ex-husband just inside the door on the floor unconscious."

"I have a six-year-old son. He was here with John." Once again Amberly felt a rising hysteria. She tore down the hallway, searching in every room of the house, but there was no sign of her son.

"We'll put out an Amber Alert on the boy," the officer was telling Cole as Amberly returned to where they stood. John was being loaded into the ambulance, and she felt that if she didn't find Max in the next minute, she was going to die.

It was at that moment her gaze fell to the floor next to the front door, and there, shining in a shaft of sunlight, was Max's necklace.

As AMBERLY FELL TO HER knees in the doorway and plucked up a silver owl on a broken piece of rawhide, Cole saw her shatter apart.

It began in the tremble that started in her hand and worked its way through her entire body. Her eyes went black, and for a moment, he feared she was going to pass out. He reached down and pulled her to her feet and into his arms, where the shaking of her body was violent.

"He…he doesn't have his necklace." The words haltingly came from her, as if jerked out by a chain of agony. "It's his protection…the owl around his neck."

"We'll find him," Cole said as he tightened his arms around her, almost frightened by the powerful tremors that swept through her. "I swear, we'll do whatever we can to find him and get him back safe and sound."

Unfortunately, Cole was out of his jurisdiction and was left powerless as the Kansas City Police Department took over. Amberly took a picture from her wallet of Max and gave it to Sergeant Mick Davis, who had taken over the scene.

Cole knew that, within minutes, the picture of the boy would be flashed on all the local television channels. But that didn't mean an instant success at locating him.

Sergeant Davis led them both into the kitchen, and they all sat at the table so they could be interrogated. Amberly told him what time Max normally got home from school; the problem was nobody could be certain when the attack had taken place. And nobody knew how long John had been unconscious after the attack.

During the interview with the sergeant, Cole held Amberly's hand tightly, hoping he was somehow helping keep the horror at bay.

It didn't take a stretch of the imagination to realize that somebody had hit John over the head and taken Max from the house. The broken necklace indicated that Max had not gone willingly. There was also no question in Cole's mind that whatever had happened in this house was related to the crimes he'd been dealing with in Mystic Lake.

Cole could tell that Amberly had gone to a very dark place inside her head as he explained to Sergeant Davis what was going on in Mystic Creek. She sat perfectly still, but he knew it was the eerie stillness that came before the damaging storm.

And then the storm exploded. She jumped out of her chair, wild-eyed and obviously half-crazed with fear. "We have to do something. We can't just sit around and do nothing. We have to go and find him. He's out there all alone…in the dark, and he's scared. He needs me."

Tears welled up in her eyes and spilled onto her cheeks as she gazed first at Sergeant Davis and then at Cole. "Please," she whispered. "Please do something."

Cole realized this was her nightmare come true, and

as her gaze held his with such pleading, such intense pain, he wanted to move the world to find Max.

"The best thing we can do right now is sit tight and let the local police work the case," Cole said with a helplessness that gnawed in his gut. "Maybe whoever took him will call."

"Why is this happening? Why would anyone want to hurt Max? Hurt John?"

These were questions that Amberly continued to ask over the next couple of hours, but nobody had any answers for her. John was conscious at the hospital but had been unable to give anyone any more information than he already had, other than the fact that Max had been standing just behind him and had been home from school for only about fifteen minutes when the attack had occurred.

As the evening turned into the darkness of night, Cole could feel Amberly's desperation. "Why don't you go lie down for a little while," he suggested when the ten o'clock hour arrived, and her face was so pale, her eyes so red from weeping that she looked as if she were terminally ill. "I'll let you know if anything happens."

She hesitated. "You promise?"

"I swear. Come on." He held out his hand and pulled her from the kitchen chair where she'd been sitting, staring at John's telephone as if willing it to ring, for the past hour.

She got up with the weariness of a broken old woman. "I should be strong," she said, her eyes once again tearing up. "I'm an FBI agent."

He pulled her against him and held her tight. "And

you're a mother, and it's okay to be a little weak right now." She stood in his embrace for several frantic heartbeats and then stepped back and nodded.

He led her down the hallway toward John's bedroom, but she stopped at the door of the first bedroom they came to. "I'll just rest in here for a few minutes," she said.

The room was obviously the place where Max slept when he was at his father's house. There was a twin bed covered in a navy spread and a desk with an intricate puzzle halfway put together on it.

Cole watched as she curled up on the bed and pulled the pillow close to her chest. As she drew a deep breath, he knew she was inhaling the very essence of her son, and as she began to cry once again, he gently closed the door and left her there, knowing at the moment he was absolutely helpless to do anything to comfort her.

Another hour passed with Cole talking to the officers on scene, listening for any reports coming in and praying that somebody someplace would find Max alive and well.

He knew the woman he loved would be broken completely if she lost Max. He understood the kind of grief she would experience, and his heart ached with his need to shield her from it.

A crime-scene unit pulled prints off the front door, but John had told them the perpetrator hadn't even stepped into the house before smashing him over the head.

One thing was certain. John Merriweather had officially dropped off the suspect list for the murders in

Mystic Lake as far as Cole was concerned. The man certainly hadn't hit himself over the head.

Through the next hour, Cole watched the Kansas City police at work and realized how much he had missed working for a bigger force. Until the murders in Mystic Lake, he'd felt stale, as if he were slowing wasting away in the small town. He'd been ready to consider making a move before the first murdered woman had been found.

But he wouldn't leave his position as sheriff of Mystic Lake until the town was safe again, until the murders had been solved and the killer was behind bars. Only then would he think about his options for his future.

At the moment his greatest concern was for the woman in the bedroom. He knew the agony that stabbed through Amberly's heart as she waited to hear about the welfare of her son. He knew that agony intimately, had experienced it when Emily had initially gone missing.

With Amberly in his mind, and nothing to do to move the investigation forward in John's attack and Max's vanishing, he quietly walked down the hallway to the room where Amberly had lain down.

He knocked softly on the door, and when there was no reply, he cracked it open, assuming the stress of the situation must have caused her to fall asleep.

Gone.

She wasn't in the bed, and the window was open, the screen displaced. Cole's heart crashed against his ribs as he raced to the window and peered out into the darkness of the night.

Had she been taken from this room as all the cops had gathered in the living room and kitchen? He looked closer at the screen. It appeared as if the screen had been removed from the inside.

If that was the case, then Amberly hadn't been taken by anyone, but rather had run away. But to where? To hunt for Max? There was no clue where to look, no trail to follow. His gut clenched as he realized the only thing she'd had with her when she'd come in here was her cell phone.

Had she received a call from the kidnapper? Didn't she realize that in all probability, the man who had taken Max was also the same man who had hung the items on her mailbox? The same man who had killed the three women in Mystic Lake?

He had to find her, but he had no idea where to begin to look. And he knew he couldn't look alone. He raced from the bedroom in search of Sergeant Davis to tell him that they didn't have just a missing boy anymore, they also had a missing woman who had been marked for murder.

# Chapter Twelve

Amberly had been in limbo, in a strange state between numbness and a screaming, silent terror when her cell phone had rung.

She hadn't recognized the caller number, but the moment she'd answered and heard Max's voice, she'd bolted up on the bed, adrenaline firing through her.

"Max! Max, are you okay? Where are you?" Frantic fear danced through her veins as she clutched the phone more tightly against her ear.

"I'm okay, Mom, but he wants you to come here to get me."

"Where, baby? Where am I supposed to go?"

Max's voice was replaced by a low snarl. "If you want to keep your son alive you come alone to the storage units at 95th and Baylor Road. If I smell a cop or anyone else with you or anywhere else in the area, then you'll never see Max again."

"Wait.... Who are you? What do you want?" But she knew she was talking to a dead line. She clicked the phone closed, her heart beating frantically and her head spinning.

Her first thought was to run to Cole, to tell him about

the call, but as the man's warning played and replayed through her head, she was afraid to risk having him anywhere near 95th and Baylor Road.

She had to save Max at whatever cost. She knew whoever held him didn't want the boy, he wanted her. She was his intended victim, and she'd do whatever she had to do in order to keep her son alive. She had her cell phone and her gun. That's all she needed.

With the stealth of a thief, she had crawled out the window and now ran down the street. Ninety-fifth and Baylor was a good two miles from John's house, even if she cut through yards and jumped fences.

Thank God she was in great physical shape and her incentive for getting where she was going couldn't have been better. The night was dark, with scarcely a moonbeam apparent. Still, she sought the shadows rather than racing beneath streetlights.

She had no idea if or when Cole might find her gone, and the last thing she wanted was for him to somehow follow her and accidentally screw things up in forcing a situation that would cost Max his little life.

She would die for her son. Of course, that wasn't her grand plan. She hoped to not only save Max but to save herself, as well. She wanted to live to see Max go to the high school prom, she wanted to be there when he chose his path in college. She needed to see the kind of man he would become, a man she knew would make her proud.

She wasn't even aware of the tears that streaked down her cheeks until she paused for a moment to catch her breath and realized the night was awash with an unnatural shine.

Angrily she swiped at her eyes, knowing she needed to remove herself emotionally as much as possible and reach for the cool calculation of a seasoned FBI agent. Still, there was no question that it was difficult to separate the professional from the terrified mother.

She began running once again, wondering who had Max and why he was after her. It didn't matter now. Whoever it was would hopefully be a dead man by the time she was finished. She'd kill him for scaring Max. She'd shoot him for hurting John. She'd make sure he never had the opportunity to kill another woman.

With this thought in mind, she picked up her pace, knowing the bomb she and Cole had discussed had exploded, and only she could control the damage.

She knew the storage facility at the location. There were between fifteen and twenty metal sheds, which were rented monthly. The place was named U-Store It, and there was no security on the premises. It was simply surrounded by a chain-link fence.

When she reached the business, she saw that the padlock on the gate had been cut off, and it gaped open in a dreadful invitation.

She held her gun tight in her hand as she slid through the small opening in the fence. There were security lights scattered about the area, and her gaze darted in all directions, seeking the man who had called her here, the man who held her child hostage.

Cocking her head, she listened, trying to discern from what direction danger would come, but she heard nothing but the sound of her own pounding heart.

Where were they? Where was the man who had

turned her world upside down? Where was Max? She felt that if another minute went by without her seeing her son, she might die. Pressure pulsed inside her stomach, rising into the back of her throat to make her feel nauseous.

"Max?" she called softly, her heart begging to hear the sound of his voice.

"Stay where you are," a deep voice said from someplace in front of her. She froze, the gun still gripped in her hand. If he took a single step from the shadows, she'd shoot him, but first she needed to know that Max was still okay.

"Where's my son?" she demanded.

"Right here." A tall man, his face hidden behind a ski mask, materialized about twenty feet in front of her, and held like a shield in front of him, Max, his eyes widened with fear.

"Hey, Max." She forced her voice to be soothing and soft. "Don't be scared. You're going to be just fine." Even as she said the words, a sense of despair swept through her. As long as the masked man held Max, she didn't dare attempt to take a shot.

"Let him go," she said, a new harshness in her voice. "He's an innocent child who has done nothing wrong."

"I'll trade him for you. Drop your gun and come closer and I'll let him go."

She hesitated. While she wanted Max free, that required two things: that she trust the man in front of her and that she relinquish the only weapon she had.

"How do I know you'll let him go?" She tried desperately to identify the man behind the mask, but the darkness made it nearly impossible.

The only thing she could tell was that he was tall and slender, and even though he was obviously attempting to alter his voice, something about it rang hauntingly familiar.

"Because I said I would," he replied. "It's you I want, not him. Throw your gun away and get down on your belly with your arms and legs outstretched. You do that, and I'll let him go right now. I swear to you."

She quickly considered her options and realized she had none. She tossed her gun as far away as she could and then got down on her belly. "Now, let him go," she said, aware of her own vulnerability and only hoping that once Max was free she would be able to somehow get herself out of danger.

Suddenly, he released Max, who stood awkwardly frozen as if unsure what to do next. "Run, Max," she cried as the masked man raced toward where she was on the ground. "Run, baby, run as fast as you can away from here. Be safe and remember always that I love you."

She trembled with relief as Max took off running and disappeared into the darkness of the night. Safe. He was safe and, even though it was late at night, he was smart and she knew he'd find somebody to help him.

At the moment, she had to focus on saving herself. She rolled over on her back as the man reached her side. She reared her legs back in hopes of kicking him, but before she could do anything to defend herself, she heard the distinctive sizzle of a Taser. The next thing she knew, the Taser pressed into the side of her neck. Sharp, electric pain shot through her and when he hit her again with it, there was blessedly nothing.

THE MINUTE COLE TOLD Sergeant Davis that Amberly was missing, he sent men out to search the streets for her. They really had no idea whether they were dealing with another kidnapping or if Amberly had left of her own volition.

Cole's biggest fear was that she had gone to meet the killer, that Max had been used as dangling bait to draw her out alone.

Dammit, why hadn't she come to him? Together they could have figured something out that would have hopefully kept both her and Max safe. But instead she'd gone out like the Lone Ranger, and he didn't know how he'd survive losing another woman he loved to a horrible death.

As he stood at the front window, flashes of visions of the dead women filled his head, and he nearly groaned aloud as he thought of Amberly so still, so lifeless and with a dream catcher hanging over her head.

Finally he could stand it no longer. He had to get outside and join the hunt. As he stepped outside, his heart felt as black as the darkness of the night.

He should have taken the opportunity to tell her he loved her. He wished he would have taken a chance to speak of his feelings for her. He wouldn't have expected anything back from her. He knew where she was in her life, what she wanted and didn't want; he simply wished he'd let her know that she was loved and his love held all the passion and desire she hadn't known before, hadn't believed existed.

He stood at the end of the sidewalk, looking first in one direction and then the other, wondering which way to go that would take him to her, the path that would allow him this time to be there to save the woman he loved.

He saw several officers down the block on the right, and so decided to go left, wishing he had more than a little bit of bloodhound in him.

The night was silent and cool, but a sweat broke out across Cole's forehead. Timing was everything and he couldn't afford to be one minute too late.

He took off at a jog, not knowing where he was headed but feeling the need to do something, anything to find Amberly and Max. He was afraid to call out for them, afraid that the killer would hear and know he was close. That might prompt things to go from bad to worse.

Each darkened house or business he passed, he paused to see if there was any sign of anything that looked out of place, that might signal danger. But there was nothing except the beat of his heart, growing more frantic by the minute.

She couldn't have gone far without a vehicle. Sergeant Davis had checked before Cole left the house to see if any taxis had been dispatched to anyplace in the area, and there had been none.

She could have called a friend for a ride, but somehow Cole didn't believe she would have done that. She wouldn't have involved anyone else in whatever drama was happening. He knew in his gut that she was alone.

And what worried him more than anything was the

fact that he wasn't even sure he was going in the right direction. As far as he knew, each footstep he took carried him farther and farther away from her and Max.

He felt as if he'd been walking forever when he saw the boy running down the sidewalk. Instantly, he recognized him as Max.

"Max!" he yelled as the boy drew closer. Cole's heart nearly stopped. If Max was out here, then where was Amberly?

"Max, I'm Sheriff Caldwell, a friend of your mom's."

These words drove Max right into Cole's arms. He burrowed his face into Cole's belly as a deep shudder worked through him. Cole held him tight. "It's okay, you're safe now," he said, reminding himself that this was a six-year-old boy who had been through who knew what kind of horror.

As he picked Max up, the little boy wrapped his arms tightly around Cole's neck. Cole's heart constricted as he felt Max's unconditional acceptance. Cole quickly used his cell phone to contact Sergeant Davis with their location so Max could be picked up by a patrol car and taken back to the house.

When Cole was finished with his call, Max raised his head and gazed up at Cole with frightened eyes so like Amberly's. "You got to find my mom. The bad guy has her and she's in bad trouble."

"I know." Cole stroked a reassuring hand down Max's back. "Max, which direction did you run from?"

Max frowned and pointed behind him. "But I jigged and jagged, and I don't know where Mom is now." Tears welled up in his eyes.

"Max, your mom told me you were really, really smart, and the two of you always play a game kind of like I Spy."

"I'm good at it, too," Max exclaimed, obviously eager to please.

"That's what your mom told me. Can you think about it now, Max? Think about where the man had you and where he might have your mom now. Tell me everything you remember about it."

Max frowned thoughtfully. "There was a fence and little houses. Is my dad okay?"

"He's fine, but he took a pretty good hit on the head, and so he's going to stay in the hospital tonight. What do you remember about the man who hit your dad?"

Once again, a little frown rode across the boy's forehead. "He had on a mask, you know, like you wear in the wintertime."

"A ski mask?"

Max nodded. "And he was wearing jeans and a blue short-sleeved shirt. He talked in a funny, low voice and pretended to be somebody else, but he was wearing the shoes he always wears when he works out in the yard, and I saw his mole when he moved his arms and his shirt opened a little."

"You know him?" Cole asked, his heart beating a thousand miles a minute. A mole? He remembered seeing a distinctive mole. "Was it your neighbor, Max?"

"Yes, it was Mr. Gershner. I don't know why he hurt my dad or why he pretended to be somebody else and took me. I pretended not to know who he was, because he was scaring me and I thought he might get mad if I told him I knew." Tears began to fill Max's eyes once again. "Please find my mom, Sheriff Cole. She needs you."

At that moment, a patrol car pulled up. As Max got into the backseat, Cole quickly told the officer behind the wheel what Max had told him and then watched the patrolman pull away.

He knew that, within minutes, the cops would be swarming Ed Gershner's place and looking for clues. In the meantime, Cole wanted to find a place with little houses and a fence before Amberly wound up stretched out somewhere with a dream catcher over her head.

AMBERLY REGAINED CONSCIOUSNESS to find herself bound at the wrists and ankles and in one of the storage units. A bare lightbulb hung from the ceiling, and through the slits of her eyes, she saw Ed Gershner working on a large dream catcher in the corner of the small room. He'd removed the ski mask that covered his face.

Shock stuttered through her at the sight of him. Ed? Friendly, neighborly Ed? Ed who played chess with John so often? What was he doing? Why was he doing this? Her head pounded with a nauseating intensity, but not so badly that she didn't realize she was in terrible danger.

He glanced in her direction. "Ah, I see you're awake. Won't be long now, just got to put the finishing touches on this dream catcher. No cheap Made In China one for you, Amberly. You should feel honored you're getting the real deal. 'Course I had to read up on how to make one of these dream catchers on the internet. Amazing, isn't it? The kinds of things you can learn from a website?"

She felt like she was staring at a man she'd never seen

before. "You killed those women in Mystic Lake?" she asked, knowing it was probably useless to scream, for there was nobody around to hear her cries.

"I did what had to be done." He wove the string with nimble fingers, creating the web of the dream catcher. "I needed you drawn away from home, to a place where nobody would suspect me. Mystic Lake was just close enough, yet far enough away from the city to accomplish what I needed. I figured the dream catchers would do the trick and get you involved, and I was right."

"But why?" She struggled with the rope that bound her hands in front of her but found it tight and well tied.

Ed stopped what he was doing and rose to his feet, his face twisted with a rage Amberly had never known before. "Why? Why? Because you have to die, that's why. It's the only way John will ever be able to live again. As long as you're anywhere on the face of this earth he'll remain nothing but a shell of a broken man."

She stared at him with horror mingling with a strange sense of wonder. For John? He was doing all this for John? "Ed, this is crazy. John will be fine. You need to let me go before anything else happens. We can get you some help."

"I don't need help," Ed scoffed. "I know just how John feels. I was married once and I loved my wife just like John loves you, with every fiber of my being. We had a son and then she got some fancy job and worked all the time. Eventually, she told me she wasn't happy in our marriage anymore and then she took my boy and left me. Just like you did to John. I know just how he feels, he's slowly dying inside from wanting you and not being able to have you."

"Then how is it going to help him if I'm gone?" Amberly asked desperately.

"Because he'll finally have to give up any hope that you'll ever get back together again. Because he'll have Max to himself without having to share him with you. He'll get on with his life because he'll have no choice. But as long as you're running in and out of his house, eating dinner with him and keeping the connection alive, you're torturing that poor man."

Amberly had never seen the light that shone from Ed's eyes, a zealous righteousness that frightened her more than anything else she'd ever seen before. He truly believed he was righting a wrong, fixing a friend he obviously cared deeply about.

He'd killed three innocent women in his mad quest to get to her. There was no reason to believe that anything she said would make him change his mind about killing her.

As he returned to his work on the dream catcher she struggled more frantically against the ropes that bound her. Somehow she had to get free.

She had to fight for her life.

She couldn't let Ed win. She refused to become nothing but a distant memory to the son she loved.

"Does John know what you're doing?" she asked, noticing that each time he talked he stopped his work on the dream catcher that would become her tombstone.

Once again, he straightened to his full height. "Of course not. John could never hurt you. As far as he'll know, you'll be just another tragic victim of the work he hated you doing. He'll mourn you for a while, but eventually, he truly will be able to move on. He'll be happy again and that's what I want for him, that's why it's necessary that you be gone."

Be gone.

Oh God, she didn't want to be gone. She wanted to live. She wanted to raise Max and find love…the kind of love Cole had shared with his wife, the kind of passion he'd shown Amberly did exist in the world.

She wanted to make love to Cole one last time, to hear the sound of his soothing voice when things were stressful. She wanted to look across his kitchen table and smile at him as they shared a morning cup of coffee.

Tears blurred her vision as she remained helplessly bound and the dream catcher was nearly finished. She knew that when it was done, the end result was that her stabbed body would be found someplace in Mystic Lake with the dream catcher hanging over her head.

"Done," Ed said as he tied the feathers into place. As he rose to his feet and smiled at her, Amberly's blood went cold as she realized there was now nothing to stop him from finishing with his final victim.

THERE WAS NO WAY FOR Cole to second-guess how Max had run from wherever he'd been held. A fence and little houses, that's what Max had said, but it made no connection in Cole's brain, and he had to remind himself that no matter how bright Max was, he was still a terrified six-year-old. A fence could mean chain link or picket, and little houses could be dog houses.

An urgency rocketed through him as he looked first in one direction and then another. How could he possibly know which way to go? It had been sheer luck that he'd run into Max at all.

At that moment, his cell phone rang. He answered to find Sergeant Davis on the other end. "We're in Gershner's house now. We've found enough evidence to link him to the murders in Mystic Lake and we also found a receipt for a storage-unit rental at U-Store It. It's on the corner of 95th and Baylor. Three months ago, he rented unit eight."

As Sergeant Davis got Cole's location, he gave Cole directions to the storage place and said he was in the process of sending officers to the scene.

As Cole clicked off, he was already running. According to Davis, he was only two blocks away. Two blocks from Amberly. There was no question in his mind that the storage unit was the kill place Gershner used, and then he transported the dead women twenty miles to be left in Mystic Lake.

He'd effectively thrown Cole off the track, making him assume the killer was local to Mystic Lake. According to Amberly, Ed Gershner played chess often with John. Ed had nearly played a perfect game here for reasons Cole didn't know. The only mistake he'd made was letting Max go, underestimating the ability of the child to recognize him despite the ski mask and his attempt at disguising his voice.

He reached the storage business and stopped at the slightly opened gate, his gaze seeking the numbering on the buildings so he could find unit eight.

Fourth building in on the left, he discerned. As he drew his gun, he approached as soundlessly as possible, praying that any patrol cars that might be on their way would not come in with sirens blaring and lights flashing.

If Amberly was still alive, then they might spook Ed into doing something deadly. Besides, if she was already dead, then all the flashing lights and screaming sirens would be for nothing.

His heart positively clenched at this thought. In fact, his guts wouldn't unclench again until he held Amberly safe and sound in his arms.

As he moved past the other units to reach number eight, he noted that the sheds had openings like garage doors in the front but each had a side entrance that was a regular door.

He also noted that a car was parked behind unit eight. He assumed it was Ed's car, ready to move his latest victim to his town. The last place Cole wanted Amberly found tonight was in Mystic Lake.

The fact that the car was still there was at least a little bit encouraging. He hadn't moved her yet, and that meant there was still hope, and he clung tightly to that hope.

There was no way he could open the rolling garage-style door at the front of the building. The minute it began to open Ed would be warned and there was no way to predict how he might act.

Cole moved to the side door and wished it contained a window so he could peer inside and see what was going on. He prayed that it was unlocked, that Gershner hadn't been expecting company or any interruptions in his macabre work. He held his gun with deadly intent, ready to do whatever necessary to save Amberly's life.

The knob slowly twisted beneath his hand at the same time he heard the sounds of cars approaching the area. Thankfully, the police had arrived as silently as possible, as if knowing their arrival might force an explosion that could end in Amberly's death.

Cole wasn't waiting for them to gather together and formulate a plan. He'd been there, done that, and with tragic results. He couldn't allow the same thing to happen to Amberly. He was in place and he was going in.

He pushed against the door and it opened soundlessly, and the scene that greeted him stopped his heart. Amberly was trussed up on the floor, and Ed was on his knees next to her, a knife raised above his head.

"Halt!" Cole screamed. Ed turned his eyes in Cole's direction, and for a minute, Cole thought the danger was over, that Ed intended to surrender without a fight. But with his eyes still locked with Cole's, the man plunged the knife downward.

Cole fired his gun and everything seemed to go into slow motion. Ed's knife hit his mark at the same time he toppled over sideways, dead from the bullet to his chest.

Amberly moaned as Cole saw the blood that quickly pooled where the knife had lodged in her abdomen. *Too late,* his brain screamed. *You were a second too late.*

He raced to her, at the same time screaming for help. He kicked Ed's body aside and slammed to his knees on the floor next to Amberly. She was quickly losing blood.

"Max?" she whispered as her beautiful face blanched of all color.

"Is fine," he replied. He worked quickly to remove the rope from her hands and then grabbed one of them in his. "Hang in there, baby. Help is on the way." He squeezed her hand tightly, as if by touch alone he could keep her with him.

He heard the shriek of a siren in the near distance and knew that it was probably an ambulance arriving on scene. "You're going to be okay," he said, fighting against the burn of tears in his eyes. He hoped, he prayed his words were right, but the amount of blood pouring out from around the knife in her stomach scared the hell out of him.

"I could really use a stick of licorice right about now," she said and then passed out.

At that moment, paramedics rushed in, and Cole stood by helplessly as they loaded her onto the gurney and took her out of the shed and toward the awaiting ambulance.

"Come on, we'll follow them," Sergeant Davis said after instructing several patrolmen to guard the area for the arrival of the crime-scene unit.

The scream of the ambulance echoed in Cole's soul as they followed behind, the sound mirroring the horror inside him.

Was she going to make it? There had been so much blood. How much could a woman lose and still live? She had to live. She had to!

As he thought of those moments when he'd first burst into the shed, he remembered that moment of hesitation before he'd fired his gun. He hadn't been prepared for Ed to act.

He should have shot the moment he entered the doorway.

He'd obviously miscalculated the situation. It was equally obvious he'd waited too long to shoot. An overwhelming despair washed over him.

Had he once again been mere seconds too late to save the woman he loved?

## Chapter Thirteen

Amberly awoke to the dawn light spilling in through the hospital window. Her first thought was for Max, and her second was for Cole.

She remembered Cole telling her that Max was safe, and although she wondered where he was at the moment, she knew wherever he was, he was okay, and that was all that mattered to her.

Even though she felt as if she'd been run over by a truck, she wasn't in the city park, dead with a dream catcher hanging over her head. Ed was dead and his reign of terror was over.

She closed her eyes, remembering those horrific moments in the shed with Gershner. He'd never hit their radar as a suspect. He'd simply been the nice man next door, who was also friends with her ex-husband.

Who could have guessed the lengths he'd go to in order to "fix" his best friend's life? She remembered him telling her about his own wife and son. Certainly Ed had been driven not just by John's demons, but also by more than a few of his own.

Cole. He'd saved her life. Tears burned in her eyes as

she thought of him, tears of gratitude and something else, something less definable.

Ed had been right about one thing. It was possible she'd been giving John mixed messages since their divorce. She often ate dinner at his house when it was convenient, after she got off work and went to pick up Max. Over the years, she'd asked him occasionally to fix a faucet or check the pilot light on the furnace.

Things needed to change. When she eventually got out of the hospital, she knew she needed to adjust the way she interacted with John. Boundaries needed to be drawn so they were both clear that she was never coming back to him, so she could truly free him to find another love.

She must have fallen back asleep, for when she awakened again, John sat next to her bed, his face somber as he stared at her with guilt-filled eyes.

"Where's Max?" she asked.

"Outside in the hallway with Sheriff Caldwell. I wanted to talk to you alone for a minute." He twisted his hands in his lap and for a moment seemed overwhelmed with emotion.

"I didn't know," he finally managed to say. "I had no idea about Ed. I had no idea about any of this. It makes me sick. It makes me wish that I'd been the one who had shot him."

She reached out a hand to him, this man who had been a friend, a lover and the father of her child. "I know," she replied.

He tightly squeezed her hand. "I'll be haunted by this until the day I die. The faces of those poor murdered women will be with me forever. Thank God your face isn't one of them." He released her hand and leaned back in his chair. "It's time I let you go."

He raked a hand through his hair and winced slightly as if the wound he'd received from Ed was still extremely painful. "I know we were never meant to be, that we were great friends who made a mistake, but during our marriage, I truly fell in love with you. I know now that I have to let go, that it's time for me to move forward with my own life."

Amberly nodded, glad that somehow this whole ordeal had put them both on the same page. "I never meant to hurt you, John, but the things we want from life, from love are very different."

"I've been a crazy fool, clinging to a wisp of smoke that was our life together, afraid to look forward and instead immersed in the past."

"Somewhere out there is a woman who will love you desperately, a woman who will want the same things you want, who will fill all your needs. Find her, John, find your happiness."

He nodded and got up from the chair. "And I think maybe you've already found yours."

She frowned at him, wondering what he was talking about. He smiled, the sad smile of goodbye. "It was his name you called out when you were coming around. If you feel up to it, I'll send him in with Max now."

"Yes, please," she said, stunned that she'd cried out for Cole in her semiconsciousness.

As John left the room, Max bounded inside and right to the side of her bed, where he leaned forward and kissed her on the cheek. "You had me worried," he said as Cole stopped just inside the door.

Her heart filled with love as she reached out a finger and traced it down the side of Max's face. "You had me worried, too."

"Mr. Gershner stabbed you and the doctor gave you new blood to make you all better. Dr. Walsh said it was a miracle that the knife didn't hit something important inside you."

"I'll be fine. You were so brave, Max."

"Sheriff Cole says I'm smart as a whip," he replied proudly. "I told him it was Mr. Gershner even though he had on a mask. He was wearing those dumb gardening shoes of his and I saw his mole once."

Pride swelled up inside Amberly. "And I see you have your owl back." She reached out and touched the talisman that once again hung around his neck.

"It came off when I was trying to get away from Mr. Gershner, but Sheriff Cole got me some new rawhide and fixed it for me."

Amberly looked at Cole, who shrugged. "It was the least I could do for the hero of the day. Now, how about you go find your dad and let me have a little alone time with your mom?"

"Okay, but I'll see ya later, right?" Max asked Cole.

"We'll see," Cole replied.

Max kissed Amberly on the cheek once again. "Hurry and get well, Mom. I want you home." He leaned forward and whispered, "And I think Sheriff Cole likes you a lot."

With these words he raced toward the door, high-fived Cole and then disappeared.

Cole stepped closer to the side of her bed. "You have no idea how glad I am to be looking into your eyes right now," he said.

She smiled. "You have no idea how happy I am to be able to stare into yours. It got a little hairy in that shed."

Cole suddenly appeared to fall apart. He stumbled into the chair next to her bed and collapsed, his eyes holding a torment that resonated inside her soul. "I thought I'd be too late. I was so afraid for you."

"But you weren't too late. I'm here and I'm alive."

"Thank God." Some of the darkness in his eyes lifted and he leaned forward, for a moment just looking at her. He finally shook his head with a small smile. "I can't figure out how we got here."

"What do you mean?" she asked.

"I can't figure out how an FBI agent I initially didn't want to work with, a woman addicted to red licorice and with a son who is as charming and bright as the day is long, got so deeply into my heart."

Amberly stared at him and she saw the depth of emotion that shone from his eyes, and she knew in the very depths of her soul that she felt those same emotions for him. But she was afraid to embrace them, afraid that somehow, someway, she would be making a mistake again, believing in something that didn't exist.

"I love you, Amberly. I love you and I want to be a part of your life, a part of Max's life."

She opened her mouth to speak although she wasn't sure what she intended to say.

In any case, he held up a hand to stop her from saying anything. "I know you told me you have no intention of starting a relationship with somebody while Max is so young. But he's smart, Amberly. He'll understand the difference between a dad and a stepdad. Heck, probably half the kids in his class at school come from broken marriages."

Amberly closed her eyes for a moment, needing to think, wanting to savor the fact that he'd told her he loved her. And she loved him. As crazy as it was, in the time they'd spent together living under his roof, she'd fallen in love with the man she'd sworn she wouldn't.

She opened her eyes again to see him watching her, waiting with a sense of both anticipation and anxiety. "I'm afraid." The words whispered from her. "I'm so afraid to believe in the kind of love I want, in the kind of love I want with you."

He reached out and touched her cheek, a light, loving touch that pierced through to her heart. "What are you afraid of?"

"I'm afraid I'll have to give up who I am to be the woman you want."

"But you are the woman I want, an FBI profiler who is bright and beautiful and loves her son and sets my heart, my very soul, on fire. Why would I want you to be anything other than what you are right now?"

"But these feelings we have for each other, how can we be sure they'll last?" She wanted to believe, she wanted him to make her believe. He was slowly chipping away at any doubts she might have, and she needed him to somehow chip away the last one.

"Because I believe in us." He reached out and took her hand in his. "You don't have to believe in love or passion that lasts forever. All you really have to do is believe in us."

The simplicity of what he said was the key that finally unlocked the last of her heart. He was right. And she did believe in him, in them together as a couple…with Max completing their family.

"I can't figure out how we got here," she said as she squeezed his hand with hers. "Who would have thought that the small-town sheriff I wanted nothing to do with would be sitting next to my bed after I'd been stabbed by a serial killer? Who would have thought that same sheriff would have my heart so completely?"

She watched his eyes lighten to the blue of sunny skies. "I love you, Cole Caldwell. I have no idea where this will take us, but as long as you provide me with plenty of red licorice, I'm in for the ride."

He leaned forward and kissed her gently on her lips and then smiled. "Fifty years from now, when we're sitting on our front porch with grandchildren running all over the lawn, you'll be sorry you only asked me to provide you with red licorice."

Her heart trembled with happiness at the thought of fifty years together with this strong, smart man, who would not only be by her side as caring support, who would not only make a perfect stepfather for Max, but would also light her nights on fire.

"And what would Granny Nightsong say about all this?" Cole asked.

Amberly smiled, thinking of the woman who had raised her. "She would say that now we will feel no rain on our heads, for we will be each other's shelter. She'd also say that we're entering into a phase of life where we will be blinded by happy sex eyes and everything will be wonderful."

Cole smiled. "I would have liked your granny Nightsong."

"She would have liked you, too." And with those words Amberly felt a rightness in her soul, as if her grandmother was smiling down at her and telling her she had finally found the path in life where her moccasins would dance forever with happiness.

# Epilogue

The May sun was warm as it beat through the car window on Amberly's body. She looked ridiculous, sitting in the driver's seat of her car in full bridal regalia.

Standing on the shores of Mystic Lake were Cole and Max and Lexie Walker and her husband, Nick, and the preacher who would make things official between Amberly and Cole.

After eight months of dating, they had decided to marry on the banks of the lake, despite the fact that Cole no longer worked as sheriff in the small town. A month earlier he had become an official member of the Kansas City police force.

She knew they were all just waiting for her to leave her car so they could get on with the ceremony, but at the moment she just wanted to gaze at the man and the child who she loved.

Both were dressed in black tuxedos. Cole had insisted they also wear red bow ties and cummerbunds for the candy that Amberly loved.

In the past eight months, her passion for Cole had never waned, her desire to talk with him and laugh with him had only grown stronger with each passing day. He'd been right. All she'd had to do was believe in them.

As she watched, Max moved closer to Cole and motioned him down to his level. Her heart constricted as Max carefully straightened Cole's bow tie.

The two had bonded, a bond that hadn't taken anything away from John but had rather given a gift to both Cole and Max. John had moved on and was dating a blonde named Susan, who loved Max and loved to cook, and Amberly had a feeling, in another six months or so, Max would be attending another wedding.

Her work kept her busy, but she was always eager to head home to her men. Speaking of eagerness, she laughed as Max waved a hand to her in obvious impatience.

Suddenly, she didn't want to sit in the car anymore. She wanted to be standing on the bank of Mystic Lake with her friends and the two men she loved more than anyone else in the world.

She got out of the car, carefully lifting the hem of the long, simple white dress. As she started toward them, Cole met her halfway, the smile on his face warming her more than a July sun could ever do.

"You ready for this?" he asked.

"Definitely," she replied. "What about you?"

"I feel like I've been waiting forever for this moment." He leaned in and captured her lips with his. Love filled the kiss, along with a dangerous passion that had her half-giddy as the kiss continued.

"Duh...you guys," Max yelled. "If you haven't noticed, we're all waiting."

Cole broke the kiss with a burst of laughter. He grabbed Amberly's hand, and they ran toward the others, toward their bright and wonderful future together.

* * * * *

# SUSPENSE

Heartstopping stories of intrigue and mystery—
where true love always triumphs.

**Harlequin**
# INTRIGUE

## COMING NEXT MONTH
### AVAILABLE MARCH 13, 2012

**#1335 CORRALLED**
*Whitehorse, Montana:*
*Chisholm Cattle Company*
**B.J. Daniels**

**#1336 COWBOY TO THE MAX**
*Bucking Bronc Lodge*
**Rita Herron**

**#1337 SECRET IDENTITY**
*Cooper Security*
**Paula Graves**

**#1338 LAWMAN LOVER**
*Outlaws*
**Lisa Childs**

**#1339 A WANTED MAN**
*Thriller*
**Alana Matthews**

**#1340 FINDING HER SON**
**Robin Perini**

# REQUEST YOUR FREE BOOKS!
## 2 FREE NOVELS PLUS 2 FREE GIFTS!

# Harlequin®
# INTRIGUE®

## BREATHTAKING ROMANTIC SUSPENSE

---

**YES!** Please send me 2 FREE Harlequin Intrigue® novels and my 2 FREE gifts (gifts are worth about $10). After receiving them, if I don't wish to receive any more books, I can return the shipping statement marked "cancel." If I don't cancel, I will receive 6 brand-new novels every month and be billed just $4.49 per book in the U.S. or $5.24 per book in Canada. That's a saving of at least 14% off the cover price! It's quite a bargain! Shipping and handling is just 50¢ per book in the U.S. and 75¢ per book in Canada.* I understand that accepting the 2 free books and gifts places me under no obligation to buy anything. I can always return a shipment and cancel at any time. Even if I never buy another book, the two free books and gifts are mine to keep forever.

182/382 HDN FEQ2

Name _____ (PLEASE PRINT)

Address _____ Apt. #

City _____ State/Prov. _____ Zip/Postal Code

Signature (if under 18, a parent or guardian must sign)

### Mail to the **Reader Service:**
**IN U.S.A.:** P.O. Box 1867, Buffalo, NY 14240-1867
**IN CANADA:** P.O. Box 609, Fort Erie, Ontario L2A 5X3

Not valid for current subscribers to Harlequin Intrigue books.

**Are you a subscriber to Harlequin Intrigue books
and want to receive the larger-print edition?
Call 1-800-873-8635 or visit www.ReaderService.com.**

* Terms and prices subject to change without notice. Prices do not include applicable taxes. Sales tax applicable in N.Y. Canadian residents will be charged applicable taxes. Offer not valid in Quebec. This offer is limited to one order per household. All orders subject to credit approval. Credit or debit balances in a customer's account(s) may be offset by any other outstanding balance owed by or to the customer. Please allow 4 to 6 weeks for delivery. Offer available while quantities last.

**Your Privacy**—The Reader Service is committed to protecting your privacy. Our Privacy Policy is available online at www.ReaderService.com or upon request from the Reader Service.

We make a portion of our mailing list available to reputable third parties that offer products we believe may interest you. If you prefer that we not exchange your name with third parties, or if you wish to clarify or modify your communication preferences, please visit us at www.ReaderService.com/consumerschoice or write to us at Reader Service Preference Service, P.O. Box 9062, Buffalo, NY 14269. Include your complete name and address.

---

HI11B

New York Times *and* USA TODAY *bestselling author Maya Banks presents book three in her miniseries* PREGNANCY & PASSION.

*TEMPTED BY HER INNOCENT KISS*

*Available March 2012 from Harlequin Desire!*

There came a time in a man's life when he knew he was well and truly caught. Devon Carter stared down at the diamond ring nestled in velvet and acknowledged that this was one such time. He snapped the lid closed and shoved the box into the breast pocket of his suit.

He had two choices. He could marry Ashley Copeland and fulfill his goal of merging his company with Copeland Hotels, thus creating the largest, most exclusive line of resorts in the world, or he could refuse and lose it all.

Put in that light, there wasn't much he could do except pop the question.

The doorman to his Manhattan high-rise apartment hurried to open the door as Devon strode toward the street. He took a deep breath before ducking into his car, and the driver pulled into traffic.

Tonight was the night. All of his careful wooing, the countless dinners, kisses that started brief and casual and became more breathless—all a lead-up to tonight. Tonight his seduction of Ashley Copeland would be complete, and then he'd ask her to marry him.

He shook his head as the absurdity of the situation hit him for the hundredth time. Personally, he thought William Copeland was crazy for forcing his daughter down Devon's throat.

Ashley was a sweet enough girl, but Devon had no desire

to marry anyone.

William had other plans. He'd told Devon that Ashley had no head for the family business. She was too softhearted, too naive. So he'd made Ashley part of the deal. The catch? Ashley wasn't to know of it. Which meant Devon was stuck playing stupid games.

Ashley was supposed to think this was a grand love match. She was a starry-eyed woman who preferred her animal-rescue foundation over board meetings, charts and financials for Copeland Hotels.

If she ever found out the truth, she wouldn't take it well.

And hell, he couldn't blame her.

But no matter the reason for his proposal, before the night was over, she'd have no doubts that she belonged to him.

*What will happen when Devon marries Ashley?*
*Find out in Maya Banks's passionate new novel*
*TEMPTED BY HER INNOCENT KISS*
*Available March 2012 from Harlequin Desire!*

# Harlequin®

## American ★ Romance®

### Get swept away with author

# CATHY GILLEN THACKER

### and her new miniseries

## *Legends of Laramie County*

On the Cartwright ranch, it's the women
who endure and run the ranch—and it's time for
lawyer Liz Cartwright to take over. Needing some help
around the ranch, Liz hires Travis Anderson, a fellow
attorney, and Liz's high-school boyfriend. Travis says
he wants to get back to his ranch roots, but Liz knows
Travis is running from something. Old feelings emerge
as they work together, but Liz can't help but wonder
if Travis is home to stay.

## *Reluctant Texas Rancher*

**Available March
wherever books are sold.**

www.Harlequin.com